JURY OF HIS PEERS

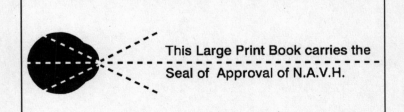

This Large Print Book carries the
Seal of Approval of N.A.V.H.

JURY OF HIS PEERS

DEBBIE MACOMBER

THORNDIKE PRESS
A part of Gale, Cengage Learning

GALE
CENGAGE Learning·

Detroit • New York • San Francisco • New Haven, Conn • Waterville, Maine • London

LIBRARY OF CONGRESS CATALOGING-IN-PUBLICATION DATA

Macomber, Debbie.
  Jury of his peers / by Debbie Macomber. — Large print ed.
    p. cm. — (Thorndike Press large print romance)
  ISBN 978-1-4104-4891-0 (hardcover) — ISBN 1-4104-4891-6
(hardcover) 1. Large type books. I. Title.
PS3563.A2364J87 2012
813'.54—dc23   2012012086

Published in 2012 by arrangement with Harlequin Books S.A.

Printed in the United States of America
1 2 3 4 5 6 7 16 15 14 13 12

To Ted Macomber, our son, the
wonderful negotiator.

ONE

There was something vaguely familiar about him. Caroline Lomax's gaze was repeatedly drawn across the crowded room where the prospective jury members had been told to wait. He sat reading, oblivious to the people surrounding him. Some were playing cards, others chatting. A few were reading just as he was. It couldn't be Theodore Thomasson, Caroline mused, shaking her head so that the soft auburn curls bounced. Not "Tedious Ted," the childhood name she had ruthlessly given him because of his apparent perfection. The last time she'd seen him had been the summer he was fifteen and she was fourteen, just before her father's job had taken them to San Francisco. It wasn't him; it couldn't be. First off, Theodore Thomasson wouldn't be living on the West Coast and, second, she would have broken out in a prickly rash if he were. Never in her entire life had she disliked anyone more.

Determined to ignore the man completely, Caroline picked up a magazine and idly flipped through the dog-eared pages. If that was Theodore, which it obviously couldn't be, then he'd changed. She would never openly admit that he was handsome back then. Attractive, maybe, in an eclectic way. But this man . . . If it was Theodore, then his eyes were the same intense blue of his youth, but his ears no longer had the tendency to stick out. The neatly trimmed dark hair was more stylish than prudent, and if Tedious Ted was anything, he was sensible, levelheaded and circumspect. And rational. Rational to the point of making her crazy. Admittedly, her own father was known to be rational, practical, discriminating and at times even parsimonious. As the president of Lomax, Inc., the fastest growing computer company in the world, he had to be.

The thought of her stern-faced father produced an involuntary smile. What a thin veneer his rationality was, at least where she and her mother were concerned. He loved his daughter enough to allow her to be herself. Caroline realized that it was difficult for him to accept her offbeat lifestyle and her choice to go to culinary school with the intent of becoming a chef, not to mention that she'd opted for a lower standard of living than what she was accustomed to. She knew he would rather see her in law school. Regardless, he supported her and loved her, and she adored him for it.

A glance at the round clock on the drab beige wall confirmed that within another fifteen minutes the prospective jurors would be free to go. Her first day of jury duty had been a complete waste of time. This certainly wasn't turning out as she'd expected. Her mind had conjured up an exciting murder trial or at least a dramatic drug bust. Instead she'd spent the day sitting in a room full of strangers, looking for a way to occupy herself until her name was called for a panel.

Fifteen minutes later, as they stood to file out of the room, Caroline toyed with the idea of saying something to the man who resembled Theodore, but rejected the idea. If it was him, she decided, she didn't want to know. In addition, she needed to hurry to the Four Seasons Hotel. Her dad had a business meeting in Seattle with an export agency, and her mother had come along to visit Caroline, a plan that was derailed when fate decreed that Caroline would spend the day in a crowded, stuffy room being bored out of her mind. Tonight the three of them were going out to dinner. From the restaurant they would take a cab, and she would see her parents off on a return flight to San Francisco.

At precisely five, she walked down the steps of the King County Courthouse and glanced quickly at the street for the bus. She swung her backpack over her shoulder and hurriedly stepped onto the sidewalk. Thick, leaden-gray clouds obliterated the March sun, and she shook off a sensation of gloom and oppression. This feeling had been with her from the moment she'd walked into the jury room, and she suspected that it didn't have anything to do with the early spring weather.

A few minutes later she smiled at the doorman in the long red coat who held open the heavy glass doors of the posh hotel. Moments later she stepped off the elevator, knocked, and was let into her parents' suite.

Ruth Lomax glanced up from the knitting she was carrying, and her eyes brightened. Her bifocals were perched on the tip of her nose, so low that it was a wonder they didn't slip completely free. "How'd it go?" she asked as she sat back down.

"Boring," Caroline answered, taking the seat opposite her mother. "I sat around all day, waiting for someone to call my name."

A smile softened her mother's look of concentration. There was only a faint resemblance between mother and daughter, which could be attributed mostly to their identical hair color. Although Ruth's was the deep combination of brown and red that was sometimes classified as chestnut,

13

Caroline's was a luxuriant shade of brilliant auburn. Other similarities were difficult to find. A thousand times in her twenty-four years, Caroline had prayed that God would see fit to grant her Ruth's gentle smile and generous personality. Instead, she had been pegged a rebel, a non-conformist, bad-mannered and unladylike — all by her first grade teacher. From there matters had grown worse. In her junior year she was expelled from boarding school for impersonating a nun. Her father had thrown up his hands at her shenanigans, while Ruth had smiled sweetly and staunchly defended her. Ruth seemed to believe that Caroline could have a vocation for the religious life and the family shouldn't discount her interest in this area. Caroline was wise enough to smother her giggles.

"You know who I thought I saw today?"

"Who, dear?" Folding her glasses, Ruth set them aside and gave her full attention to her daughter.

"Theodore Thomasson."

"Really? He was such a nice boy."

"Mom!" Caroline exclaimed. "He was boring."

"Boring?" Ruth Lomax looked absolutely shocked and smiled gently. "Caroline, I don't know what it is you have against that boy. You two never could seem to get along."

"Being with him was like standing in a room and listening to someone scrape their nails down a blackboard." Irritated, Caroline yanked the backpack off and tossed it carelessly aside. "I suppose you're going

to want me to wear a dress tonight."
Her usual jeans and T-shirt had been
a constant source of aggravation to
her father. However, tonight Caroline wanted to keep the peace and do
her best to please him.

Ruth ignored the question, her look
thoughtful as she set aside her knitting. "He was always so well-
mannered. So polite."

" 'Stuffy' is the word," Caroline
interjected. "It's the only way to
describe a fifteen-year-old boy who
takes dancing lessons."

"Lots of people take dance lessons,
dear."

Caroline opened her mouth to ob-
ject, then closed it again, not wishing
to argue. As a boy, Theodore had
been so courteous, charming and full
of decorum that she'd thought she

would throw up.

"He was thoughtful and introspective. As I recall, you were dreadful to him that last summer."

Caroline shrugged. Her mother didn't know the half of it.

"Sending him all those mail-order acne medications was outrageous." She wasn't able to completely disguise a smile. "C.O.D. at that. How could you, Caroline?"

"I wanted him to know what it was like not to be perfect in every way."

"But his skin was flawless."

"That's just it. The guy didn't have the common decency to have so much as a pimple."

Slowly, her mother shook her head. "And you had pimples and freckles."

"Don't forget the braces."

"And he teased you?"

Caroline tossed her jacket over a chair without looking at her mother. "No, he wouldn't even do that. I'd have liked him better if he had."

"It sounds to me as if you were jealous."

"Oh, really, Mother, don't get philosophical on me. What's there to like about a kid whose favorite television program is *Meet the Press?* Believe me, there's nothing to envy."

Although her mother didn't comment, Caroline felt her frowning gaze as she busied herself, pulling out a skirt and sweater from the backpack. "What ever became of him, Mom, do you know?"

"The last I heard, he was working for the government."

"Probably the Internal Revenue Service," Caroline said with a mocking arch of her brow.

"You may be right."

That secret smile was back again, and Caroline wondered exactly what her mother was up to. "He's the type of guy who would relish auditing people's tax returns," Caroline mumbled under her breath, running a brush through her thick hair until it curled obediently at her shoulders.

"By the way, Caroline, your father and I are definitely getting you a bed for your birthday."

"Mom, I don't have room for one."

"It's ridiculous to pull that . . . thing down from the wall every night. Good grief, what would you do if it snapped back into place in the middle of the night?"

Caroline smiled. "Cry for help?" It wasn't that she didn't appreciate the offer, but her apartment was small enough as it was. Having a fold-up bed was the most economical use of the limited space. The apartment was cozy — all right, snug — but its location offered several advantages. It was close to the Pike Place Market and the heart of downtown Seattle. In addition, her school was within walking distance. As far as she was concerned, she couldn't ask for more.

"You need a decent bed," her mother argued. "How do you expect to find a job if you don't get a good night's rest?"

"I sleep like a baby," Caroline returned, hiding a smile. "Now, about dinner tonight. Would you prefer to take a taxi to meet Dad, or are you brave enough to try the backseat of my scooter?" She only suggested this for shock value. The scooter was safely tucked away in the basement of her apartment building.

"Your scooter?" Ruth's voice rose half an octave as she turned startled eyes toward her daughter.

"Don't worry, I can see you'd prefer the taxi."

Since Charles Lomax was tied up later than expected in a meeting, Caroline and her mother took a taxi directly to La Mer, an elegant Seattle restaurant that overlooked the ship canal connecting Lake Union with Puget Sound. A large stone fireplace with a crackling fire greeted them. As they checked their coats, Caroline glanced around the expansive room, seeking her father's burly figure. When she caught sight of two men rising from a table in the middle of the room, her heart dropped. Next to her father was the same man she'd seen in the jury room, and something told her it really was Theodore Thomasson. So this was the reason for her mother's strange little smiles. Everything fit into place now. This business deal with the export outfit was somehow linked to Theodore.

"Ted, how nice to see you again." Ruth Lomax embraced him and stepped back to study him. "You've grown so tall and good looking."

"The years have only enhanced your beauty." He looked beyond Ruth to Caroline. "I wondered if that was you today."

So he had noticed her. Caroline's throat felt scratchy and dry. On closer inspection, she was forced to admit that Theodore had indeed changed.

The boyish good looks of fifteen had matured into strikingly handsome sculpted features that were the picture of both strength and character. Theodore Thomasson was attractive enough to cause more than a few heads to turn. And Caroline was no exception. Her bemused thoughts were interrupted by his deep male voice, which was as intriguing as his looks.

"Hello, Caroline." His eyes moved with warm appraisal from her mother to rest solidly on her. Then the friendliness drained from the brilliant blue gaze as they sought and met hers. "It's good to see you again, Hot Stuff."

Caroline fumed at the reference to that last summer and the incident she sincerely hoped her parents never connected with her. With an effort, she managed to shrug lightly and smile. "Touché, Tedious Ted."

With a hearty laugh, Charles Lomax pulled out a chair and seated his wife. Before Ted could offer her the same courtesy, Caroline seated herself.

"I see you're not intimidated by my daughter," her father told Ted with a smile.

Silently, Caroline gritted her teeth. Theodore Thomasson wasn't getting the best of her that easily. Her chance would come later.

Her gaze was drawn to the huge windows that provided an unob-structed view of the ship canal. Sail-boats, their sails lowered, glided past, with the brilliant golden sun setting in the background.

Inside the restaurant, the tables,

covered in dark red linen, were each graced with a single long-stemmed rose. La Mer was rated among the best restaurants in Seattle. She had never eaten here before, but the elegance of the room assured her that no matter what the food was like, this was going to be a special treat.

"I understand you work for the government. The Internal Revenue Service, is it?" Caroline asked Ted with mock-sweetness, then turned away to study the elaborate menu. She hoped the dig hit its mark.

"And exactly what is it that *you* do?" From beneath dark brows he observed her with frank interest. She noted that he hadn't answered her question. Although his eyes didn't spark with challenge, there was an uncompromising authority in the set of his jaw that wasn't the least bit to Caroline's liking.

Her mother spoke up quickly. "Caroline graduated cum laude from —"

"I'm training at the Natalie Dupont School," Caroline interrupted. Unsure that he would recognize the name of the nationally famous culinary school, she added, "I'm a chef — or I will be shortly. I've just completed a year's apprenticeship." Her father had had a difficult time accepting the fact that she'd chosen a career as menial as cooking. Ambition and hard work had driven Charles Lomax to the top of his profession. Caroline didn't doubt that she would have to work just as hard making a name for herself, but though he rarely argued the point with her, she knew her father didn't agree.

The aggressive vitality in Ted's eyes demanded that she look at him. "So you didn't grow up to be a fireman," he said with a smile.

Caroline felt a cold sweat break out across her upper lip. Her family knew nothing of the fireworks display she had rigged outside his bedroom the night of July third.

"No." She forced her voice to sound as innocent as possible, as if her memory had blotted out that unfortunate chain of events that had set the balcony on fire.

"Shame," he responded casually. "You displayed such a talent for pyrotechnics."

"What's this?" her father asked, his gaze swinging from Caroline to Ted.

"Nothing, Dad." She gave him her

most engaging smile. "Something from when we were kids."

Ted's mouth quirked in a half smile.

Caroline tilted her chin and haughtily returned his gaze. "You were such an easy target," she whispered.

"Not anymore, I'm not."

Smoothing the starched linen napkin over her lap, Caroline gave him a cool look. "I never have been able to turn down a challenge."

"Am I missing something here?" her father demanded.

"Nothing, Dad," Caroline answered. "Tell me, Theodore, what brought you to Seattle? I always thought you'd think of Boston as home."

"Most people call me Ted."

"All right . . . Ted."

"Seattle's a beautiful city. It seemed

a nice place to live."

"Are you always so vague?" Caroline's voice was sharp enough to cause her mother to eye her above the top of the menu. Unbelievable! She actually found Theodore — Ted — as irritating now as she had when they were teenagers. Worse, even.

"Only when I have to be," he taunted lightly, doing a poor job of disguising a smile.

Caroline itched to find a way to put him in his place and was surprised at the intensity of her feelings.

The meal was an uncomfortable experience. Countless times Caroline found her gaze drawn to Ted. In astonishment, she noticed the way his eyes would warm when they rested on her mother and immediately turn icy cool when they skimmed over her.

He didn't like her, that much was obvious. But then, he had little reason to do anything but hate the sight of her.

Through the course of the conversation, Caroline learned that though Ted might have worked for the federal government at one time, but he didn't now. From the sound of things, her guess had been right and he was employed by the export company that had brought her father to Seattle. She didn't want to ask for fear of sounding interested.

The meal was as delicious as she'd been led to believe it would be, so she focused on that and made only a few comments, spoke only when questioned and smiled demurely at all the appropriate times.

"So you two are both serving jury

duty this week," her father said after an uncomfortable pause in the conversation. "What a coincidence."

Caroline's and Ted's eyes met from across the table.

"I call it bad luck," Caroline answered. She toyed with the last bit of baked potato as she dropped her gaze.

"And neither of you was aware that the other lived here?"

"No." Again it was Caroline who answered, then mumbled under her breath that moving to California was looking more appealing by the minute. If she expected a reaction from Ted, he didn't give her one. He'd heard her, though, and one corner of his mouth jerked upward briefly. Somehow she doubted that the movement was in any way related to a smile.

"Never served on a jury myself," her father continued. "Don't know that I ever will."

"It must have been twenty years ago when I was called. You remember the time, don't you, Charles?" Ruth chimed in, and detailed the account of the robbery trial on which she'd sat.

When Caroline did chance a casual look Ted's way, she was rewarded with a slightly narrowed gaze. Outwardly, he looked as if he hadn't a care in the world and was thoroughly enjoying himself. She couldn't imagine how. He couldn't help but feel her obvious dislike. Occasionally she would catch him studying her and flush angrily. His pleasant, amused expression never varied, which only served to aggravate her more. He should be the uncomfortable one. Instead, he exchanged pleasantries with her parents, then spoke affectionately of his own family. When the bill was presented, Ted insisted on paying, and in the same breath offered to drive her parents to the airport.

"But I thought I was taking you," Caroline objected.

"Your father and I can hardly ride on the back of your scooter," her mother said with a teasing glint in her eye.

"Scooter?" Ted repeated with a curious tilt of his head.

Caroline bristled, waiting for a cutting remark that didn't come.

"It's the most economical way of getting around," she supplied and granted him a saccharine smile.

"It's a shame my daughter has to be economical about anything," her father said with a rumbling chuckle. "She's taking this cooking business seriously. Living within her means. I give her credit for that."

Caroline had to bite her tongue to keep from reminding him that she was training to be a chef, not a short-order cook. A year of schooling, plus another year's apprenticeship, proved that this was serious business. In four years of college she hadn't worked as hard as she had in the last two years.

"It will work out fine to have you drop us off at the airport," her father continued.

"I'll take a taxi from here," Caroline said. The thought of getting stuck alone with Ted Thomasson on the return ride from the airport was more than she could tolerate.

"Nonsense. I'll see you home," Ted said smoothly, one dark brow rising arrogantly, daring her to refuse.

"Theodore, you were always so polite," Ruth said, smiling at her daughter as if to point out that Caroline had indeed misjudged him all these years.

Personally, Caroline doubted that. He might have matured into a devilishly handsome man, but looks weren't everything.

From the restaurant, the foursome returned to the Four Seasons Hotel so the Lomaxes could collect their luggage. The ride to the airport took an additional uneasy twenty minutes. Caroline buried her hands deep inside her pockets as she walked down the concourse at Sea-Tac International. She dreaded the time when she would have to face Ted without her parents present to buffer the conversation.

Her father and mother hugged her goodbye and Caroline promised to email more often. In addition, they promised to pass on her love to her older brother, Darryl, who lived in Sacramento with his wife and two young sons. All the while they were saying their farewells, Caroline could feel Ted's eyes studying her.

He didn't say anything until her parents had disappeared into the security line.

"The cafeteria's open."

She cast him a curious glance. "We just ate a fantastic meal. You couldn't possibly want another."

One brow arched briefly. "I'm suggesting coffee."

"No thanks."

"Fine." His long stride forced her to half walk, half run in order to keep up with him. By the time they were in the parking garage, she was straining to breathe evenly. Not for anything would she let him know she was winded.

The ride back into the city was completed in grating silence. It wasn't until they were near the downtown area that she relayed her address. Even then, she said it in a mechanical monotone. Ted glanced at her briefly and his fingers tightened around the steering wheel. This was even worse than she'd imagined.

When he pulled into a parking lot across from her apartment, turned off the engine and opened the car door, butterflies filled her stomach. "I didn't invite you inside," she said indignantly.

"No," he agreed. "But I'm coming in anyway." A thread of steel in his voice dared her to challenge him. In disbelief, she watched as his slow, satisfied smile deepened the laugh lines at his eyes. Too bad. Whatever he had in mind, she wasn't interested.

"Listen," she said, striving for a cool, objective tone. "If you want an apology for what happened that summer, then I'll give you one."

Ted acted as if she hadn't spoken. Agilely, he stepped out of the car and slammed the door closed. Caroline climbed out on her own before he could walk around to her side. Opening a lady's car door was something he would obviously do, given the kind of man he was.

She stopped and looked both ways before stepping off the curb. A hand at her elbow jerked her back onto the sidewalk. "What are you doing?" he demanded.

Caroline stared at him speechlessly. "Crossing the street," she managed after a long moment.

"The light's this way."

Ted hadn't changed, not a bit. Good grief, he didn't even jaywalk. She clenched her jaw, hating the thought of him invading her home.

"Did you hear what I said earlier?" she asked. "I owe you an apology. You've got one. What more do you want?"

His hand cupped her elbow as they stopped at the traffic light. She pulled her arm free, angrier with her body's warm response to his touch than the fact that he'd taken her arm.

The light changed, and they crossed the street. The brick apartment building was four stories high. Caroline's tiny apartment was on the third floor. All the way up the stairs, she tried to think of a way of getting rid of Ted. She realized that arguing with him wasn't going to do any good. She might as well listen to what he had to say and be done with it.

The key felt cool against her fingers as she inserted it into the lock. A flip of the light switch bathed the room in a gentle glow.

Standing just inside the apartment, Ted made a sweeping appraisal of the small room. Caroline couldn't read the look in his eyes. Hooking her backpack over the doorknob, she turned to him, hands on her hips. "All right," she said in a slow breath. "What is it you want?"

"Coffee."

Seething, she marched across the room to the compact kitchen. With anyone else she would have ground fresh-roasted beans. As it was, she brought down one earthenware mug, dumped a teaspoon of instant coffee inside and heated the water in the microwave.

"Satisfied?" she asked sarcastically as she handed him the steaming mug.

"Relatively so." His half smile was maddening.

Pulling out a chair, he sat and looked up at her standing stiffly on the other side of the narrow room. "Have a seat."

"No thanks. I prefer to stand."

He shrugged as if it made no difference to him and blew on the coffee before taking a tentative sip.

Stubbornly, Caroline crossed her arms in front of her and waited.

"I want to know why," he said at last.

"Why what?" she snapped.

"Why do you dislike me so much?"

"Have you got a year?"

"I have as much time as necessary."

"Where would you like me to begin?" Her voice was deceptively soft, but her feelings were clear. By the time she was finished, his ears would burn for a week.

"That last summer will do." He still refused to react to the antagonism in her voice.

"All right," she said evenly. "You

were perfect in every way. Honest, sincere, forthright. What kind of kid is that? Darryl and I had stashed away fireworks for weeks, and you acted as if we'd robbed a bank."

"They were illegal. You're lucky you didn't blow your fool head off. As it was —"

"See." She pointed an accusing finger at him. "If you didn't want any part of it, that was your prerogative, but tattling to my dad was a spiteful thing to do. It's that goody-goody attitude I couldn't tolerate," she continued, warming to the subject.

Ted looked genuinely taken back. "What? I didn't say a word to your family."

Caroline's lungs expanded slowly. Ted Thomasson probably hadn't stretched the truth in his life. She couldn't do anything but believe him. "Then how did Dad find out I had them?"

"How am I supposed to know?" His eyes nearly sparked visible blue flame.

"At least he never found out how I got rid of them."

"What were my other crimes?"

Uneasy now, Caroline shrugged weakly.

"Well?" he demanded.

"You wouldn't go swimming with me." The one afternoon she'd made an effort to be nice, Ted had flatly rejected her offer of friendship.

A brief smile touched his eyes. "True, but did you ever ask yourself why?"

"I don't care to know. What was the matter? I was trying to be nice. Were you afraid I was going to drown you?"

"Knowing your past history, that was a distinct possibility."

"It wasn't my fault the brakes on that golf cart failed."

"Don't lie to me, Caroline. You never hid what you thought of me before."

Guilt colored her face a hot shade of red. "Okay, I'll admit it. I never liked you. And I never will." She crossed her arms again to indicate that the conversation was closed.

"Why didn't you like me?" he asked softly, setting his coffee aside. The chair slid back as he suddenly stood.

Caroline pinched her mouth tightly closed. When he moved so that he loomed over her, she clenched her jaw.

"Why?" he repeated.

"I . . . just didn't . . . that's all."

She detested the way her voice shook.

"There's got to be a logical reason." His eyes cut through her.

"Your hair was always perfectly trimmed." Her gaze locked with his in a fierce battle of wills. "It still is," she added accusingly.

"Yours is still the same fiery red." As if he couldn't resist, he reached out and wove a thick strand around his index finger. "I remember the first time I saw it and wondered if your hair color was the reason you were so hot-tempered."

"A lot you know." Her voice gained strength and volume. "My hair is auburn."

He laughed softly, as if he found her protestations amusing.

"You've probably never done anything daring in your life," she went on. "You were always afraid of one thing or another. You're the most boring person I ever met."

"And you're a hellion."

"But I've never bored anyone in my life," she snapped defensively.

"Neither have I. You simply didn't give me the chance to prove it to you." He released her hair to slide his fingers around her nape in a slow, easy caress.

Caroline drew in a sharp breath and tried to shrug his hand free. A crazy whirl of sensations caused her stomach muscles to tense.

"Take your hand off me." She grabbed his arm in an effort to free herself.

He ignored her protests. "Was there anything else?"

"You . . . took dancing lessons."

Nodding, he laughed softly. "That I did. Only I hated them more than you'll ever realize."

"You — never wanted to do anything fun." Desperately her mind sought valid reasons for her intense dislike of him and came up blank.

"I want to do things now," he drawled in a voice that was barely perceptible. Ever so slowly, he lowered his mouth to hers.

Mesmerized, her heart pounding like the crashing waves upon a sandy shore in a storm, Caroline was powerless to stop him. When he fitted his mouth over hers, she made a weak effort by pushing against his chest. No kiss had ever been so sweet, so perfect, so wonderful. Soon her hands slid around his neck as she pressed her soft figure to his long length, clinging to him for support.

When they broke apart, she dropped her arms and took a staggering step backward. The staccato beat of her heart dropped to a sluggish drum roll at the wicked look twinkling in Ted's eyes. He'd wanted to humiliate her as she'd done to him all those years ago. And he'd succeeded.

"I bet you didn't think kissing 'Tedious Ted' could be so good, did you, Caroline?"

Two

Caroline woke with the first light of dawn that splashed through her beveled-glass window. The sky was cloudless, clear and languid. Her first thought was of Ted and her overwhelming response to his kiss. Silently, she seethed, detesting the very thought of him. To use sensory attraction against her was the lowest form of deceit. He'd wanted to humiliate her and had purposely kissed her as a means of punishment for the innocent crimes of her youth. And what really irritated her was that it had been the most sensual kiss of her life. Her cheeks burned with mortification, and she pressed cool palms to her face to blot out the embarrassment. Ted Thomasson was vile, completely without scruples, and that was only the tip of the iceberg as far as she was concerned.

The morning was chilly, but Caroline had her anger to keep her warm. If she'd disliked Ted Thomasson at fourteen, those feelings paled in comparison to the intensity of her feelings now. Yet she had to paint on a plastic smile and sit in the same room with him today, pretending she hadn't been the least bit affected by what had happened. If she were lucky, she would be called out early for a trial, but at the rate her luck was running, she would end up stuck sitting next to him for the next four days.

The brisk walk to the King County Courthouse helped cool her indignation. She bought a cup of coffee from a machine and carried it with her into the jury room. The bailiff checked off her name and gave her a smiling nod. Caroline didn't pause to look around, afraid Ted would see her and think that she was seeking him out. As far as she was concerned, if she saw him in another eighty years it would be a hundred years too soon.

The coffee was scalding, and she set it on a table to cool while she reached for a magazine — an outdated copy of *Time.* Flipping through the pages, she noted that the stories that had captured the headlines six months ago were still in the news today. Little had changed in the world. Except Ted — he'd changed. His aggressive virility had captured her attention from the minute they'd stepped into the restaurant. Forcibly, she shook her head to reject the thought of him. She detested the way he'd invaded her mind from the minute she'd climbed out of bed.

She caught a movement out of the corner of her eye and turned to see. Ted stood framed in the doorway of the large, open room. He wore an impeccable three-piece gray suit with leather shoes. Italian, no doubt. After spending a restless day lounging in the jury room, almost everyone else had dressed more casually today. She herself had slipped on dark cords and an olive-green pullover sweater. But not Mr. Propriety. Oh, no, his long legs had probably never known the feel of denim. Angrily she banished the image of Ted in a pair of tight-fitting jeans.

"Morning." He claimed the empty chair beside her. "I trust you slept well. I know I did."

Wordlessly, she took her cup of coffee and moved to a vacant seat three chairs down.

Without hesitating, Ted stood and followed her. "Is something wrong?"

Despite her anger, she managed to make her voice sound calm and reasonable. "If you insist on pestering me, then you leave me no option but to report you to the bailiff."

"Did I pester you last night, Caroline?" he asked in a seductive drawl that sent shivers racing down her spine.

"Yes." She felt like shouting but made an effort and kept her voice low.

"Funny, that wasn't the impression I got."

"You're so obtuse you wouldn't recognize a —"

"Your response to me was so hot it could have set off a forest fire."

She drew a rasping breath. She tried and failed to think of a comeback that would wipe that mocking grin off his face.

"From the time we were children, I've disliked you," she murmured, her gaze fixed on her coffee. "And nothing's changed."

His soft chuckle caught her off guard. She'd expected something scathing in retaliation, but certainly not laughter. In hindsight, she realized that Ted had probably never raised his voice to a woman.

"That's not the impression you gave me last night," he taunted.

Seething, Caroline closed her eyes. Her mind groped for a logical explanation of what had happened. She'd only had one glass of wine with the meal, so she couldn't blame her response on the influence of alcohol. Telling him that her biorhythms were out of sync would make her sound like an idiot. "Knowing that you've always been perfect in every way, I don't expect you to understand a momentary lapse of discretion on my part," she finally said.

"I don't believe that any more than you do," he said with cool calm.

Crossing her arms in front of her, she refused to look at him. "Fine.

Believe what you want. I couldn't care less."

"You care very much," he returned flatly.

Pinching her mouth tightly closed, she refused to be drawn further into the conversation.

"You intrigue me, Caroline. You always have. I've never known anyone who could match your spirit. You were magnificent at fourteen. With that bright red hair and freckles dancing across your nose, I found you absolutely enchanting."

Slowly, she appraised him, searching each strongly defined feature for signs of sarcasm or derision. She was so taken aback by the gentle caress of his voice that any response died in her throat. "How can you say that?" she managed at last. "I was horrible to you."

"Yes," he chuckled, "I know."

"You should hate me," she said.

"I discovered I never could."

The bailiff began reading the names on the first panel of jurors, and Ted paused to listen, along with the hundred and fifty other people seated in the room. Periodically during the day, the court sent requests down to the jury room and names were drawn in a lottery system, and this same hush fell over the crowd every time.

Caroline's name was one of the first to be called. At last, she thought, she was going to see some of the action. A few seconds later she heard Ted's name. They were being called along with several others for the same trial.

They were led as a group into an upstairs courtroom and seated outside the jury box. Caroline sat down on the polished mahogany pew, uncomfortably distracted by the knowledge that Ted was behind her. Their conversation lingered in her mind, and she wanted to free her thoughts for the task that lay before her. She looked up and noticed that several people were studying the potential jurors. The judge, in his long black robe, sat in the front of the courtroom, his look somber. The attorneys were at their respective tables, as was the defendant. She found her gaze drawn to the young man who stared at the group with a belligerent sneer.

Everything about him spoke of aggressive antagonism — his looks, his clothes, the way his eyes refused to meet anyone else's. His slouched posture, with arms folded defiantly across his chest, revealed a lack of respect for the court and the legal proceedings. The defense attorney leaned over to say something to him, but the defendant merely shrugged his shoulders, apparently indicating that he didn't care one way or the other. What an unpleasant man, Caroline thought, holding back her instant feelings of dislike. Above all, she wanted to be impartial and, if she were chosen for the jury, base her decision on the evidence, not the look of the defendant.

The judge spoke, announcing that the defendant, Nelson Bergstrom, was being tried for robbery and assault. Twelve of the panel members were led to the jurors' box. Caroline was the last to be seated in the first row. A series of general questions was addressed to the prospective jurors. No one answered out loud, instead raising their hands if their response was positive. No one on the jury knew the defendant personally. Several had heard of this case through the media, since there had been a string of similar late-night assaults against female clerks. No one had an arrest record of their own. Three members had been the victims of crime. After the general questions, each juror was interviewed individually.

The attorney who approached the box smiled at Caroline, who thought that Ted was dressed more like a lawyer than this lanky guy with an easy grace and charming grin. One by one, he asked the prospective jurors specific questions regarding friends, attitudes and feelings. When he was finished, his opposite number stepped up and had his own questions for them. Neither attorney challenged Caroline for cause, but she was surprised at the number of available jurors who were dismissed for a variety of reasons, none of which seemed important to her. The two lawyers went through the first twelve-member panel and called for another. In the end, she, Ted and eleven others were chosen. The thirteenth member was an alternate who would listen to all the testimony. However, he would be called into the deliberation only if one of the jurors couldn't continue for some reason, a procedure intended to prevent the need for a retrial.

The trial began immediately, and

the opening statements made by each attorney filled in the basic details of the case. A twenty-three-year-old clerk, a woman, had been robbed at gunpoint at a minimarket late one night shortly before Thanksgiving. Terrified, the woman handed over the money from the till, as requested. The thief then proceeded to pistol whip her until her jaw was broken in two places. Although the details of the crime were relayed unemotionally, Caroline felt her throat grow dry. The defendant revealed none of his feelings while the statements were being made. His face was an unyielding mask of indifference and hostility, a combination she had never thought was possible. Again and again she found her gaze drawn to him. In her heart she realized that she fully believed Nelson Bergstrom was capable of such a hideous crime. As soon as she realized that she was already forming an opinion, she fought to cast it from her mind.

By the end of the first day, Caroline's thoughts were troubled as the jurors filed from the courtroom. Serving on a jury wasn't anything like what she'd anticipated. When she'd been contacted by mail with her dates of service, her emotions had been mixed. This was her first free week after completing her apprenticeship, and she'd hated the thought of spending it tied up in court. Now that she was sitting on a case, the reality of the crime genuinely distressed her. The victim was no doubt sitting in the courtroom. Caroline hadn't picked her out of the small crowd, but she knew she had to be there. Absently she wondered how the poor woman could endure the horror of that night.

"Are you all right?" Ted asked her once they hit the steps outside the courthouse.

"Of course," she said, struggling to sound offhand. It had been another stroke of bad luck to have Ted on the same trial. She hadn't seen him in ten years, and now, in a mere two days, he had become an irritating shadow she couldn't shake.

The jury had been warned against discussing any of the details of the case with each other. Caroline yearned to ask Ted what his impression of the proceedings had been but bit back the words. She felt strangely, unaccountably melancholy. Bemused, she frowned at the brooding sense of responsibility that weighed her down. This was only the beginning of the trial, and already she felt intimately involved with the victim *and* the defendant.

"Let's go have a drink," Ted said, taking her elbow. "We both need to relax."

She felt as if she'd been anesthetized and didn't argue — another clear sign of her confusion.

It wasn't until they entered the bar that Caroline realized she was acting as docile as a lamb being led to the slaughter.

"The Tropical Tradewinds?" She raised questioning eyes to Ted.

"You look like you're in the mood for something exotic."

She shook her head and released a slow sigh. Honestly, it was just like Ted to bring her somewhere like this. Oh, the Tropical Tradewinds had a wonderful reputation, but it certainly wasn't her style. She doubted that a place like this even carried something that didn't call for at least six ingredients. "What I'm in the mood for is a good ol' fashion beer."

"Fine, I'll order you one," he returned, pressing a hand to the small of her back as he directed her toward a vacant table. Politely, he held out a chair for her, and, struggling to hold her tongue, she took a seat. She never could understand why men found it necessary to seat women. They seemed to assume that the weaker sex was incapable of something as simple as sitting without assistance. Obviously Ted felt she needed his help, and this once she would let it pass; she simply wasn't in the mood to get into a fight with him.

The waitress arrived, and before Caroline could open her mouth, Ted placed their order. Unable to restrain her reaction, her blue eyes clashed with his as the waitress headed to the bar.

"What did I do wrong now?" he asked quietly, his gaze studying her.

"Does it look as if I've lost control of my tongue?"

"No, but I was hoping." His devilish grin served only to aggravate her further.

"Incidents like these irritate the hell out of me," she said, crossing her legs.

"Incidents like what?"

"Pulling out my chair, ordering my

drink, opening a car door. Do I honestly look so helpless?"

"A gentleman always —"

"Can it, Thomasson. I'm not up to hearing a dissertation on the proper behavior of the refined adult male."

"Caroline," Ted replied curtly, "in this day and age a man is often placed in an unpleasant position. Half the time I don't know which a lady prefers. If I don't hold out her chair, I'm considered a creep, and if I do, I'm a chauvinist. It's a no-win situation."

"I suppose you'll pay for this with a gold-plated credit card, too."

"What's that got to do with anything?" His mouth hardened with displeasure, then softened into a faint smile as their waitress approached. She placed two thick paper coasters on the round tabletop, and set down

Caroline's beer and Ted's scotch.

One look at his drink and Caroline rolled her eyes.

"Now what?" The acid in his voice was scathing.

"You're drinking scotch?"

"I would have thought that much was obvious when I ordered." He started to say more, then stopped, as if he couldn't trust himself to speak.

Remorse brought a flush of guilt to Caroline's cheeks. Ted was only trying to be nice, and her behavior was inexcusable. "Listen, Ted, I apologize for . . . I don't mean to be so rude. It's just that we're so different. We'll never be able to agree on anything."

Her casual apology didn't seem to please him either.

"If it's any consolation, you turned out about a thousand times better than I ever imagined," she continued. More than his good looks prompted the statement. He really wasn't the bore she would have expected. He was a little too concerned with propriety, but some women would appreciate that quality. Not her, but someone else.

His blue gaze frosted into an icy glare as he stared at her.

"See," she murmured triumphantly, catching his look. "You and I grate against each other. I prefer a beer out of a can."

"And I enjoy the finest scotch."

"Exactly." She supposed she should be pleased that he agreed with her so readily. "I'm a morning person." She looked at him questioningly.

"I do my best work at night."

"Baseball is my favorite sport." She

leaned back in the chair and took a drink of the cold beer. It helped ease the dryness in her throat. "I suppose you enjoy polo."

"No." He shook his head and lowered his gaze to his glass. "Curling."

"Of course." She did her best to disguise a smile.

"I'm certain that if we looked hard enough we'd discover several common interests."

"Such as?" Her look was skeptical.

The beginning of a smile added attractive brackets to the corners of his mouth. "You're a chef, and I definitely enjoy eating."

"Well, you didn't deny working for the Internal Revenue Service at one time, but I don't enjoy paying taxes."

"Caroline," he muttered with obvious control, "I was employed for a brief time by the federal government, but that was years ago. I'm in exports now."

He regarded her steadily with sky-blue eyes. He really had wonderfully expressive eyes. The thick lashes were the same dark color as his hair. If she allowed it, she realized, she could watch him forever. She lowered her own eyes, fearing what he might read in them.

"We should concentrate on the interests we share."

"Good idea." She scooted closer to the table. "Do you play cards?"

"I'm a regular shark."

"Great." Perhaps the real problem between them was something as simple as her own attitude. They were bound to find several things to enjoy about each other if they looked hard enough.

"How about bridge?" he asked.

"Bridge?" Caroline spat out the word. "I hate it. It's the most boring game in the world. I like poker."

Ted stared at her in amazed disbelief. "Okay, we'll forget cards."

"What about music?" At the cynical arch of his brow, she added, "My tastes may surprise you."

"Everything about you surprises me."

"Ha!" She was beginning to enjoy this. "I already know your tastes. You appreciate Michael Buble, I bet."

"Talented guy," Ted agreed.

"And," she paused to give some thought to his tastes, "I imagine you enjoy some of the early rock and roll stars like Buddy Holly. I'll throw in the Kingston Trio just to be on the safe side. In addition, I'm sure you're crazy about classical."

"Very good." His smile was devastating. "I'm impressed."

"All right." Gesturing with her hand, she offered him the opportunity to add his own speculations regarding *her* musical tastes. "Do your worst — or best, as the case may be."

He chuckled, and amusement flickered across his features. "I couldn't begin to venture a guess. You are a complete enigma to me and always have been. That's what makes you such an enchantress."

Caroline's smile was filled with confident amusement, sure she was about to surprise him. "I adore Mozart, Gene Autry and Billy Joel."

"Not Kermit the Frog?"

"Don't tease," she replied cheerfully. "I'm serious."

"So was I."

For the first time that evening, she felt completely at ease. She lounged back in the chair and tucked one foot under her. "Shall we dare venture into television?"

"Speaking of which, did you see the recent PBS special on fungus?"

For a moment she assumed he was teasing, but one look assured her that he was completely serious. All her energy was expended in an effort not to laugh outright. "No, I must have missed that. I was watching old reruns of *I Love Lucy*."

"From the sounds of this, perhaps it would be best to move on to something else."

"What was the last book you read?"

He shifted uncomfortably and took a sip of his drink. "I think we should skip this one, too."

"Ted," she whispered saucily, "don't tell me you're into erotica."

"What? *No,*" he responded emphatically, obviously uneasy. "If you must pursue this, I recently finished Homer's *Iliad.*"

Caroline pushed the errant curls from her forehead. "In the original Greek?"

He nodded.

"I should have known," she muttered under her breath. Absolutely nothing about this man would surprise her anymore. He was brilliant. She wanted to resent that fact, but instead she found a grudging respect taking root.

"What about you?"

"I enjoy romances and science fiction and Dick Francis."

"Dick who?"

"He writes horse-racing mysteries. You have to read him to believe how good he is. I'll lend you some of his books if you'd like."

"I would."

Caroline offered him a bright, vivacious smile as she polished off her beer. "You realize we haven't found a single interest we share."

"Does it matter?" Just the way he said it sent a chord of sensual awareness singing through her, igniting an answering reprise within her heart. She couldn't believe that she was looking at Theodore Thomasson and hearing music. That was something reserved for novels. Romances. No, science fiction.

"Caroline . . ."

She shook her head to clear her thoughts. "Sorry, what were you saying? I wasn't listening."

"I was asking you to have dinner with me."

"Here?"

His look was one of tolerant amusement. "No, you choose."

"Great." Mentally she discarded her favorite Egyptian restaurant and asked, "Is Italian okay?"

"Anything's fine."

She sincerely doubted that but managed to hide her knowing grin. "There's a seafood place within walking distance if you'd rather."

"The choice is yours," he said.

"Don't be so accommodating," she said, raising her voice. "There's only so much of that I can take."

With a wide grin, Ted stood. She noted that he didn't offer her his hand as she got out of her chair, a small courtesy for which she was disproportionately grateful.

Dusk had settled over the city as they moved onto the sidewalk. Streetlights were beginning to flicker around them.

"Your dad said you went to college. What's your degree in?"

"Biochemistry." She watched the surprise work its way over his features and marveled at the control he exhibited.

"Biochemistry," he repeated in bewilderment. "And now you're in culinary school?"

"Yup. I felt that of all the majors I could have chosen, biochem would be the most value to me."

Confusion shone from his expressive eyes. "I don't think I care to follow your line of reasoning."

"It's not that difficult," she answered brightly. "You see, Dad never was thrilled with my ambitions in the kitchen. I am, after all, his daughter, and he didn't feel I was aiming high enough, if you catch my drift."

"I understand."

"So instead of constantly arguing, we made an agreement. I'd go to college and get my degree, and in exchange he'd continue to support me while I went to culinary school afterwards."

"That sounds like a fair compromise. Did you come up with it?"

"Who, me?" She pressed her palm to her breast. "Hardly. I was too involved in defending my individual rights as a human being to see any solution. Mom was the one who suggested that course of action."

"But why did you choose biochemistry?"

"Why not?" she tossed back. "I'd like to think of myself as a food scientist. There's a whole world out there that has only been touched on."

"I'm surprised your father didn't insist on sending you to Paris, if you were so sure that cooking was what you wanted to do."

"He offered." The frustration remained vivid in her memory. "Only the best for his little girl and all that rot. But I didn't want to go overseas. The Natalie Dupont School here in Seattle is one of the best, and it offers a focus on baking. I'd like to focus my efforts in the area of breads.

The average person looks at a loaf and thinks of sandwiches or toast. I see lipids, leaveners, proteins and biological structures. Yeast absolutely fascinates me."

"Obviously I'm a less complicated soul. What fascinates me most is you."

The tender look in his eyes nearly stopped her heart. "Me?" She stared at him, hardly believing the pride and wonder in his gaze. His blue eyes were full of warmth, and he was smiling at her with gentle understanding in a way she never would have suspected.

"Have you noticed your sense of timing is several years off?"

"My what?" Caroline's look was bewildered. "How do you mean?"

"At a time when most women are

happy to get out of the kitchen, you're battling your way in."

Smiling, she nodded and placed her hand in the crook of his arm. Within the span of one day, she felt as if Ted and she had always been the closest of friends. True, they didn't share a lot of common interests, but there was a bond between them that was beyond explanation. The knowledge stunned her, and she paused, wanting to speak, but not knowing what to say or how to say it.

Caroline knew when he lowered his head that he intended to kiss her, and her eyelids slowly fluttered closed with eager anticipation. When nothing happened, her eyes shot open to discover him staring down at her. Reluctantly, it seemed, he kissed the top of her head and took her hand as they continued to stroll down the street.

Mortified, she felt the embarrassment extend all the way to her hairline. Seconds earlier they'd experienced a spiritual communication that left her breathless with wonder, and now . . . The traffic light changed, and a long series of cars whizzed past. In a flash, Caroline understood that as much as he might want to, Ted wouldn't kiss her on a busy Seattle street. Not with the possibility of them being seen.

Their meal was wonderful. It could have been the wine, but she doubted it. In spite of their many differences, they found several subjects on which they shared similar opinions. They both enjoyed chess and Scrabble and, most surprisingly, shared the same political affiliation, though Ted's sense of humor was more subtle than her own. By the time they left the Italian restaurant, Caroline couldn't remember an evening she'd enjoyed more. She'd laughed until her stomach ached.

Ted's hand at the back of her neck warmed her spine as they lazily strolled toward her apartment.

"I had a good time," she said casually, reaching over and entwining her fingers with his.

"Don't sound so surprised." His chin nuzzled the crown of her head.

"I can't help it. Darryl would keel over if I told him I'd spent an enjoyable evening with you."

She basked in the warmth of his slow, easy smile.

"I never did understand how your

parents could possibly have two such completely different children. Darryl's exactly like his father, and you . . . well, it's just hard to believe you're his sister."

Caroline pulled her hand free. Disappointment and anger burned through her. "I've already apologized for my childhood bad behavior. You're right, I treated you terribly. I tricked you. I lied about you. I nearly burned the house down in an effort to undermine you. But that was twelve years ago." Whirling, she marched away.

"Caroline?" Hurried footsteps sounded behind her. "What did I say?"

"You know exactly what you said." She tried to walk faster, her pace just short of an outright jog.

"I *don't* know," he countered. His hand on her shoulder stopped her. Turning her around, he held her shoulders while his bewildered gaze roamed her face. A frown drew his thick brows together. "I've hurt you."

"What you said about not knowing how . . . how I could possibly be Darryl's sister, when you know good and well that I'm not."

A stunned look drained the color from his face. "Are you saying you're adopted?"

Her narrowed, fiery glare answered the question for him.

"That's impossible," he whispered.

THREE

"Just what exactly do you mean by that remark?" Hands on her hips, Caroline stared into his face.

"You look —"

"Like my mom? No I don't."

"The hair —"

"That's the only thing, but otherwise we're nothing alike. Mom's gentle, patient, forgiving. Every day of my life I've wanted to be exactly like her. I've honestly tried, but I'm —"

"Stubborn, quick-tempered and

often impertinent," Ted supplied for her.

She opened her mouth to argue, then thought better of it. "Yes," she admitted, then rammed her hands inside the pockets of her cords and began shuffling backwards. "Thank you for tonight, I'm sorry it has to end this way."

"Come on, Caroline. I can't be blamed for an innocent mistake. I didn't know."

"You do now."

"What difference does it make?"

"Think about it," she snapped. "You're a smart man. You'll figure it out."

"Since we're tallying your faults, you can add unreasonableness to your growing list. I've never met a more frustrating woman."

Turning, Caroline made her escape, running up the three flights of stairs that led to her apartment. She knew she was behaving badly, but she couldn't help it. From childhood, Ted had been Mr. Prim-and-Proper and she had ridiculed him for it. But that wasn't the real reason she'd disliked him so intensely. The truth was, he was everything she wanted so badly to be.

If she were even half as refined as Theodore Thomasson, her mother would have been so proud. If only she could have maintained high grades and managed to stay out of trouble, everything would have been so grand. But no matter how hard she tried or how many promises she made, she simply couldn't be something she wasn't. Her temper flared with the least provocation, her poise was as fragile as fine china, and her self-confidence was shattered by every grade school teacher who was unfortunate enough to have her in class. Perhaps she could have accepted herself more readily if her mother hadn't been so tolerant and forgiving. She'd wanted to cry and beg her mother's forgiveness for every minor blunder, but her mother would never allow that. She loved her daughter exactly the way she was. Often when Caroline was sent to her room without dinner by her father — the ultimate punishment — her mother would smuggle in fruit and cookies. More times than Caroline could count, her mother had calmly intervened between her and her father. Amazing as it was, she shared a strong relationship with her mother. There wasn't anything Caroline felt she couldn't share with her. No mother could have been more wonderful.

Each year, on Caroline's birthday, her mother told the story of how she'd longed for a daughter. Darryl was her son and she loved him dearly, but she wanted a daughter and had prayed nightly that God would smile upon her a second time and grant her another child — a girl. After five years it became apparent that she wouldn't have more children, and they'd decided to adopt. On their first visit to the caseworker, Ruth had seen a picture of a fiery-haired, two-year-old toddler and known instantly that this was just the little girl she wanted. At that point in the tale her father always interrupted to add that the caseworker had discouraged them from adopting the tiny hellion. But Ruth had persisted until the caseworker relented and brought the four of them together for the first time. Usually at this point her brother, Darryl, would insert that the first time he'd seen Caroline, she'd bitten him on the leg. He claimed she'd marked him for life and had the scar to prove it. So she had been adopted into this family who loved her in spite of her rambunctious behavior. For their love, Caroline would be forever grateful, but in her heart she would never really feel a part of them. Theodore Thomasson was a constant reminder of exactly how different she was. Next to him, her imperfections were magnified a hundred times.

An air of expectancy hung over the proceedings early the following morning. The jury was seated in a closed room adjacent to the courtroom, but Caroline arrived in time to see the defendant being brought into the court and seated. Again she noted his apparent lack of concern. It was almost as if he didn't care what the jury or anyone else thought. He was purposely making himself unlikable, and she couldn't understand that.

She stepped into the room reserved for the jury and sat beside a grandmotherly woman who paused in her knitting and said hello.

"I want to talk to you," Ted whispered.

Caroline smiled apologetically to

the older woman, who had already gone back to her knitting. "I don't know that man. Would you kindly tell him that if he continues to pester me, I'll be forced to report him to the bailiff?"

"I can't understand what's the matter with these young men today." The metal needles clicked as they wove the fine strands of yarn in and out. She had been knitting through the entire proceedings the day before, and Caroline had dubbed her Madame La Farge.

Now Madame La Farge turned and gifted Ted with what Caroline was sure was a scathing look. "Kindly leave this young lady alone."

"Caroline . . ." Ted ground out her name, his voice ringing with frustration.

Ignoring him, she scanned the faces of her fellow jurors, thinking that they resembled a fair cross section of society. All the men were dressed casually, except Ted, who wore a pin-striped suit. There were an electrician, a real estate broker, an engineer and others whose occupations Caroline couldn't recall. The other four women on the jury were all middle-aged.

"All rise, this court is now in session," the bailiff announced, and a rustling sounded in the jury room as those in the courtroom rose to their feet.

Within minutes the door opened and the jury was led in and seated. The prosecutor stood to present his case, calling several witnesses. The defendant, Nelson Bergstrom, had been tried and found guilty of assault and robbery five years before, and had been on parole only six weeks at the time of the minimarket robbery. His parole officer testified that Nelson had been living within ten blocks of the market. Another witness testified that he had seen Nelson at the store the day before the robbery.

The arresting officer followed with his report.

The next witness, Joan MacIntosh, was called. Caroline saw a young woman slowly enter the courtroom. Obviously nervous and shaky, Joan cast a pleading glance to the large man who had walked in with her. He gave her an encouraging smile and squeezed her hand, then took a seat. From the fear in the woman's eyes, Caroline realized that Joan MacIntosh must be the woman who had been assaulted. She was petite, barely five feet, with a fragile, delicate look. If she weighed over a hundred pounds, it would have been a surprise. The woman was terrified, that much was obvious. She hesitated once and glanced back. The man who'd come in with her nodded reassuringly several times, and Joan squared her shoulders before continuing forward.

The scene was poignant. Whatever physical harm had been done her had apparently healed, but it was obvious that the psychological damage had been far greater. Caroline looked at Joan and was overcome with sympathy. They were close in age, and from the address, Caroline knew they didn't live more than three miles apart. It could have been her instead of Joan who had been treated so brutally.

After being sworn in, Joan took the witness stand. Following a series of perfunctory questions, the prosecutor leaned against the polished banister. "Joan, to the best of your ability, I'd like you to tell the court the events of the night of November twenty-third."

Joan's voice had been weak and wobbly, but as she began speaking, she gained confidence and volume. "I was working as a clerk for the market for only two weeks. There — really isn't much to tell. I was alone, but that didn't bother me, because there had been a steady stream of customers in and out most of the night."

The prosecutor gave her an encouraging smile. "Go on."

"Well . . . it must have been close to eleven, and things had slowed down. I noticed someone hanging around outside, but I didn't think much of it. A lot of kids hang around the store."

Caroline noticed that Joan's hands were tightly clenched, and that a tissue she was holding was shredded.

"Anyway — he . . . the man who had been outside, came into the store. He went to the back by the refrigerator unit. I assumed he was going to buy beer or something. But when he approached the register I noticed that he had a ski mask over his face. And he had a gun pointed at my heart." Joan's voice grew weak as she remembered the terror. Briefly, she closed her eyes.

"Go on, Joan."

"He . . . he didn't say anything to me, but he pointed the gun at the cash register. I wanted to tell him he could have everything, but I couldn't talk. I was . . . so scared." She blinked, and Caroline could see tears working their way down her face. "I would have done anything just so he wouldn't hurt me."

"What happened next?"

"I opened the till to give him the money." She hesitated and bit her trembling bottom lip. "He told me to put all the money in a sack. I did that — I even gave him the change. I was so frightened that I dropped the bag on the counter. All the time I was praying that someone would come. Anyone. I didn't want to die. . . . I told him that over and over again. I begged him not to hurt me." Her voice cracked, and she placed a hand over her mouth until she'd regained her composure. "Then he looked inside the sack and told me it wasn't enough."

"What did you tell him?"

"I said I'd given him all the money there was and that he could take anything else he wanted."

"How did he react to that?"

"He told me to give him my purse, which I did. But I only had a few dollars, and that made him even angrier. He started waving the gun at me. I begged him not to shoot me. He told me to get more money. He shouted at me over and over that he needed more money. Then he started hitting me with the gun. Again and again he hit my face, until I was sure I'd never live through it. The pain was so bad that I wanted to die just so it would stop hurting."

Caroline could barely make out the words, because Joan was sobbing now. The man who'd accompanied her stood and clenched his fists angrily at his sides. The bailiff pointed to him, indicating that he should sit down again. The man did, but Joan's testimony was obviously upsetting him.

Caroline doubted that anyone could remain unaffected by the details. Joan MacIntosh was a delicate young woman who had been brutally attacked and beaten for less than twenty dollars. Caroline felt that any man who could beat someone so much smaller and virtually defenseless — or anyone, for that matter — should rot in prison.

After a few more questions, the prosecutor stepped back and sat down, and the defense attorney came forward. Joan sat up and eyed him suspiciously.

"Can you describe to the court what the man who attacked and robbed you looked like?" he asked in a calm, cool voice.

"He . . . he was average height, about a hundred and sixty pounds, dark hair, dark eyes. . . ."

"Did you ever get a clear view of his face?" the defense attorney pressed. "I noted in your testimony that you claim that the man who beat you had been hanging around outside the store."

"Well, I . . ."

"It seems to me that you would have had ample opportunity to clearly see his face," he pressed.

"Not entirely. He wore a ski mask."

"What about before, when he was outside the store? When he first came in?"

"He . . . he averted his . . . I only saw his profile."

"Before you answer the following question, Ms. MacIntosh, I want you to think very carefully about your answer. Is the man who attacked you in this courtroom today?"

Caroline's eyes flew from Joan to the defendant. Nelson Bergstrom was sneering at the young woman in the witness box, all but challenging her to name him.

"Is that man in the courtroom today?" the defender repeated.

"I . . . think so."

The attorney placed the palms of his hands on the bannister and leaned forward. "A man's entire future is at stake here, Ms. MacIntosh. We need something more definite than 'I think so.'"

"Objection." The prosecutor vaulted to his feet.

Caroline listened as the two men argued over a fine point of law that she didn't entirely understand, and then the defense attorney went back to questioning Joan. When the cross-examination was complete, the judge dismissed the court for a one-hour lunch break.

After the defendant was led away, the courtroom emptied into the hall. Ted was standing outside the large double doors waiting for Caroline.

She paused, and their eyes met and held. Listening to the morning testimony had drained her emotionally and physically. She waited for the rising tide of resentment she'd so often experienced in his presence, but none came. After last night she realized that it would be best to keep their relationship strictly impersonal.

His look was long and penetrating, as if he were reading her thoughts. A full minute passed before he spoke. "Are you going to talk to me, or am I going to be forced to send you notes through your bodyguard with the knitting needles?" The quiet tenderness in his deep voice softened her struggling resolve to remain detached. He hadn't done anything to provoke her, not really. She could hardly blame *him* for the circumstances of her birth.

"We can talk," she said, and looped the long strap of her purse over her shoulder. "Really, I should be the one who does the talking."

Ted touched her elbow, guiding her in the direction of the elevator. As if forgetting himself, he quickly lowered his hand. Caroline managed to hide a secret smile. He was trying so hard to please her. She simply couldn't understand why he would want to go to that much trouble.

"Once again, I find myself in the position of having to apologize to you," she began as they paused on the outside steps. "I realize now that you didn't know I was adopted. In fact, I find it a compliment that you hadn't guessed years ago."

"Apology accepted," he said, smiling down at her. Together they walked down the long flight of stairs that led to the busy sidewalk. "I don't know what made you so angry, but then, I've given up trying to understand what makes you tick."

In spite of herself, Caroline laughed. "Dad said the same thing to me when I as ten."

"I'm a slow learner," Ted admitted and slipped an arm around her shoulder. "It took me until late last night to realize that I'll probably never understand you. With that same thought came the realization that you mattered enough to me to keep trying."

"Why would you even want to?" His reasoning was beyond Caroline. And he thought *she* was difficult to comprehend!

His expression softened, and he looked at her with an unbearable gentleness. He traced a finger along the delicate curve of her jaw and down her chin to linger at the pulse that hammered wildly at the base of her neck. The muscles of her throat constricted, and she swayed involuntarily toward him.

"I'm not exactly sure why," he admitted, slowly shaking his head. "Maybe it's as simple as the magnetic attraction between opposites."

"No one is more opposite than you and I."

"That is something we can definitely agree on," he said, and led her across the street.

"Where are we going?"

"There's an excellent French restaurant a couple of blocks from here."

There was a guarded edge to his voice as he studied her. "You don't like French food." It was more statement than question.

"It's fine. It's just I'm not very hungry. I was thinking of walking down to the waterfront and ordering clam chowder from Ivar's."

"Listening to the testimony this morning bothered you, didn't it?"

They had been strictly warned against discussing any of the details of the trial. Fearing that once she answered she would blurt out the opinions she was already forming, Caroline simply nodded. "I could feel that poor woman's terror."

"I don't think there was a person in the room who wasn't affected by it," he agreed.

She dragged her eyes from his,

wanting to say more and knowing she didn't dare. "Jury duty is so different from what I thought it would be. Monday morning I was hoping I'd get on an exciting murder trial. Today I'm having difficulty dealing with the emotional impact of an assault and robbery. Can you imagine what it's like for the jury on something as horrible as a murder case?"

"I don't think I want to know," Ted murmured with feeling.

They strolled down to Seattle's busy waterfront. The smell of salt water and seaweed drifted toward them. A sea gull squawked as it soared in the cloudless blue sky and agilely landed on the long pier beside the take-out seafood stand.

Caroline insisted on paying for her own lunch, which consisted of a cup of thick clam chowder, a Diet Pepsi and an order of deep-fried mushrooms. Ted ordered the standard fish and chips.

They sat opposite each other at a picnic table. As much as she tried to direct her thoughts into other channels, her mind continued to replay the impassioned testimony she'd heard that morning.

"Are you seeing anyone?" Ted's question cut into her introspection.

"Pardon?"

"Are you involved with someone?"

Caroline stared at him and noted that his dark brows had lifted over inscrutable blue eyes. That he didn't like asking this question was obvious.

But even if he didn't like asking it, ask it he had, and she wasn't all that pleased to be answering it. "Not this month," she said flippantly.

"Caroline," he said with a sigh. "I'm serious."

"So am I. Romance is a low priority right now. I'm more interested in finding a job."

He didn't even make a pretense of believing her. "Who was he?" he asked softly.

"Who?"

"The man who hurt you."

She laughed lightly. "And people say *I* have a wild imagination."

"I'm not imagining things. The minute I asked you about a man, a funny, hurt look came over you."

Still? Caroline expelled her breath in a slow, even sigh. Clay had broken up with her over two months ago, but the memory of him was still as painful as it had been the night they'd finally split. She opened her mouth to deny everything, then realized she couldn't. The only person who knew the whole story was her mother. Caroline had enjoyed being with Ted the last couple of days, but that didn't mean she was up to sharing the most devastating experience of her life with him. And yet she couldn't stop herself from speaking.

"His name was Clay," she began awkwardly, repeatedly running her index finger along the rim of her cup. "There's not much to say, really. We dated for a while, decided we weren't suited and went our separate ways."

Ted's smile was sympathetic but firm. "You're not telling me the half of it."

"You're right, I'm not," she confirmed hotly. "Who said you had the right to butt into my personal life? What makes you think I'd share a painful part of my past with you? Good grief, I'm not even sure I like you. At any minute you're likely to turn back into 'Tedious Ted.' " Tension and regret were building within her at a rapid rate. She regarded him with cool disdain. How dare he put her in this position? "What would you know about love? In your orderly existence, I doubt that you've . . ." She stopped before she said something she would regret. "I didn't mean that," she finished, feeling wretched.

He took her hand, his fingers folding around hers. "I'm sorry I asked."

She refused to lower her gaze, although it demanded every ounce of her willpower. "It was over several weeks ago. . . . I don't know why I reacted like that."

"Are you still in love with him?" he asked meaningfully.

Caroline pasted a smile on her mouth and glanced his way with a false look of certainty. "No, of course not." Not if she could respond to Ted's kiss the way she had. Her overwhelming reaction to him had been a complete shock. His mouth had claimed hers and it was as if Clay had never existed. However, that night, that kiss, had been a fluke. It had been so long since a man had kissed her with such passion that it was little wonder that she'd responded.

An uneasy silence stretched between them, until Ted slid off the bench and stood. "We should think about getting back."

"Yes, I suppose we should," she replied stiffly. She rose. Pausing, she turned her eyes toward the long row of high-rise structures, her gaze seeking the courthouse. A sinking sensation landed in the pit of her stomach. "I have the funniest feeling about this case," she murmured, and stopped, surprised that she'd spoken out loud.

Ted was giving her a look that said he was experiencing the same mixed feelings. "Come on, let's get this afternoon over with." He reached for her hand, and Caroline had no objection.

The jury entered the courtroom using the same procedure as they had that morning and sat down to hear testimony.

The defending attorney presented

his defense by recalling two of the morning's witnesses for an additional series of questions.

Caroline kept expecting Nelson Bergstrom to take the stand in his own defense, but it soon became obvious that he wasn't going to be called. It didn't take much to understand why. With his attitude, he would only hurt his own chances.

The closing arguments were completed by three o'clock, and the jury entered into deliberation at three-fifteen. By the time they were seated at the long jury table, Caroline's thoughts were muddled. She didn't know what to think.

The first order of business was electing a foreman. The first choice was Ted, which surprised her. She decided to attribute it to his crisp business suit, which made him look the part. He declined, and the engineer was elected.

A short discussion followed, in which points of law were discussed, and then they went on to the evidence. This was the first time any of the jury members had been given the opportunity to discuss the trial and voice their opinion.

"If looks count for anything, that young man is as guilty as sin," Madame La Farge said, her knitting needles clicking as her fingers moved with an amazing dexterity.

"They don't," Ted said in a flat, hard voice.

"Everything that was said today, every piece of evidence, was circumstantial." Caroline felt obliged to state her feelings early. From the looks of those around her, everyone else had already made up their minds.

"As far as I see it," the real estate agent inserted, "it's an open-and-shut case. That man repeatedly hit that poor girl, and nobody's going to convince me otherwise."

"None of the money was recovered."

"Of course not," Madame La Farge inserted, planting her needlework on the tabletop. "That boy was desperate. Obviously he spent it as fast as he could on drugs. Crack, no doubt. One look at that man and anyone can tell he's an addict. No one in his right mind would act the way he did otherwise."

"He was wearing the same jacket as the assailant. What more evidence do we need?" someone else piped in.

"He was wearing a Levi's jacket, which is probably the most popular men's jacket in America. We can't convict a man because of a jacket," Caroline added heatedly.

"He lived in the neighborhood, and he had been seen there the day before."

"I know," Caroline agreed, backing down. She looked at the faces studying her and realized that she could well be standing alone on this. "I am as appalled by what happened to Joan MacIntosh as anyone here. I would like to see the man who did this to her rot behind bars. But even stronger than my sense of righteousness is the fact I want to be certain we don't punish the wrong man."

"That's everyone's concern," the foreman told her.

"The evidence is overwhelming."

"What evidence do we really have?" Ted asked.

"She identified him," Madame La Farge commented as if she were discussing the weather, pausing to cover her mouth when she yawned. "I really would like to be home before five today. Do you think we could have a vote?" She directed her question to the foreman.

"I'm not ready," Caroline insisted. "And she *didn't* identify him," she added, contradicting the older woman's statement. "Joan MacIntosh said that she *thought* it was him. In her mind there was a reasonable doubt. There's one in mine, too."

Half the room eyed her balefully. An hour later Caroline was convinced they would never reach a unanimous decision. Caroline felt taxed to the limit of her endurance. The only other person in the room who had voiced the same doubts as she was Ted.

"I have misgivings, as well," he said now.

"Maybe these two are right," one woman said softly. Groans went up around the room.

"Are we going to let that . . . that beast walk out of here after what he did?" The real estate agent rolled his pencil across the table in disgust. "Come on, folks. The sooner we agree, the sooner we can go home."

"Listen, everyone," Ted said, squaring his shoulders as he sat straighter. "I'm as anxious to get home as the next person, but we can't rush these proceedings."

A half hour later the judge sent in a note, asking if they were anywhere close to reaching a verdict.

"See?" the real estate agent fumed. "Even the judge is shocked at how long this is taking. We should have been out of here an hour ago."

The foreman wrote out a reply and sent it back to the judge. Within fifteen minutes they were dismissed and told to return in the morning.

This time it was Caroline who was waiting in the hallway for Ted. Her hands were clenched at her sides as waves of intense anger washed over her. He paused and grinned at her, but she waited until they were alone to speak, then struggled to make her voice sound normal. "Just what do you think you're doing?"

"Doing?" he asked in confusion.

"Listen, I don't need anyone to defend me, so step off your shining white horse and form your own opinions. I don't appreciate what you're doing." She caught his startled look and ignored it.

"What are you talking about?"

"This case. Don't you think I know what you're doing? It's that chauvinistic attitude of yours. The fanatical gentleman in you who refuses to let me stand alone against the others."

A look of sorely tried patience crossed his face. "Believe what you will, but I happen to share your sentiments regarding the case."

"Ha!" she snapped.

The controlled fury in his eyes was enough to knock the breath from her lungs. She noted the red tinge that was working its way up his neck and the tight, pinched look of his mouth. "I can assure you, Miss Lomax, that I consider it a miracle that we share any opinion. I would appreciate it, however, if you'd afford me the intelligence to decide for myself how I feel about this case without making unwarranted assumptions."

Suddenly drowning in resentful embarrassment, she murmured, "If I've misjudged your actions, then I apologize."

"From the time you were a girl your mouth has continued to outrun your brain," he said with deadly calm. "I have endured your anger, your lack of manners, even your temper. But I have no intention of being further subjected to your stupidity."

Hot color invaded her cheeks, and Caroline experienced an unwanted pang of misgiving. "Maybe I spoke out of turn."

The look he gave her would have frozen rainwater. Without a word, he pivoted sharply and left her standing alone in the wide hall. She pushed the curls from her face and forcefully expelled her breath. Tendrils of guilt wrapped themselves around her heart. She'd done it again. And this time she'd messed it up good. Ted wouldn't have anything to do with her now. She should be glad, but instead she discovered a sense of regret dominating her thoughts. Maybe they could settle things after the trial. Maybe, but from his look, she doubted it.

FOUR

"Has the jury reached a verdict?" the stern-faced judge asked the foreman. The engineer rose awkwardly to his feet. The courtroom was filled with tense silence. Every face in the crowded room turned to stare expectantly at the twelve men and women sitting in the jury box.

The foreman shifted uneasily, casting his gaze to his nervously clenched hands. "No, we haven't, Your Honor."

Low hissing whispers filled the room. Caroline lifted her gaze to the young victim and watched angry defeat dull her eyes as she cupped her trembling chin. Joan MacIntosh gave a small cry before burying her face in the shoulder of the man Caroline suspected was her husband.

After long, tedious hours of holding her ground, repeating the same arguments over and over until she longed to weep with frustration, Caroline was unsure about the evidence and how she should vote. As much as anyone, she wanted the man who had so brutally attacked Joan MacIntosh punished. But as much as she yearned for justice, she also needed to feel sure that she was sending the right man to prison.

Holding her ground hadn't been easy. Neither she nor Ted had wavered from their earlier stand, although others had made some persuasive — and heated — arguments. Still, Caroline couldn't change what she believed simply because someone else saw things differently. A mistrial was the worst possible outcome, as far as the courts were concerned. The jury members had been warned earlier that if it were possible to make a decision, one should be made. But since they couldn't agree unanimously, there had been no choice but to return to the courtroom and the judge.

"What was the vote?' The deepening frown in the judge's weathered face revealed his displeasure.

"Ten to two," the foreman returned, pausing to clear his throat. "Ten of us felt the defendant was guilty, the other two," he hesitated and swallowed, "didn't."

The judge studied the twelve jury members, then called for a jury poll.

When her turn came, Caroline slowly, reluctantly, said, "Not guilty." Unable to meet the judge's penetrating glare, she lowered her eyes. Unexpectedly her gaze clashed with the surly defendant's. A ghost of a grin hovered around his mouth, as if he were silently laughing at everything that was going on around him. Caroline was reminded again that Nelson Bergstrom had already been proven capable of such a hideous crime.

"You leave me with no option but to declare a mistrial." The judge spoke in a solemn voice, and it seemed to Caroline that his tone was sharp and angry. "The defendant is free on ten thousand dollars bond. A new court date will be set at the end of the week. The jurors will return tomorrow to fulfill the rest of their obligation to serve."

Joan MacIntosh burst into tears, her sobs reverberating against the hallowed walls. A dark shroud of uncertainty wrapped around Caroline's tender heart. She felt tears prickle the corners of her eyes, and she pinched her lips tightly together as the gavel banged down and the jurors were dismissed.

It seemed as if everyone in the room was accusing her with their eyes. She wanted to stand by Ted, lean on him for support, but since their last argument, he had barely spoken to her. Even her greetings had been met with clipped, disinterested replies. Ted wasn't the sort to get angry easily, and to his credit, he'd put up with a lot from her over the years. But when she'd questioned his integrity, she had committed the unforgivable. A hundred times since, she'd wished she could have pulled back the thoughtless words, but the truth was, defending her decision was just the kind of thing Ted would think chivalrous. If anything, she was pleased they shared the same opinion. If ever she needed a friend, it had been today, standing against her the fellow members of the jury. Yet even when their decisions concurred, they were treating each other as enemies.

The line of accusing faces didn't fade when Caroline and Ted entered the wide hallway outside the courtroom. The man who had sat with Joan MacIntosh was waiting for them, as were photographers from the local newspapers.

The moment Caroline appeared, the presumed Mr. MacIntosh started spewing a long list of obscenities at her with the venom of a man driven past his endurance. At first she was stunned, too shocked to react, and then she couldn't believe anyone would talk to her that way. She had been called some rotten things in her life, but nothing even close to this.

"I didn't mean to upset you," she pleaded, yearning desperately to explain. "I'm so sorry," she went on, "but if you only understood why I voted the way I did —"

She wasn't allowed to finish, as another tirade of harsh, angry words broke across her explanation. Bright lights flashed as the press took in the bitter scene.

"Caroline," Ted said sharply, coming to her side. "It won't do any good to reason with him. Let's get out of here."

"But he needs to understand. Everyone does," she insisted, turning toward the reporters. "Ted and I agonized over the decision."

"Ted?" one reporter tossed back at her.

"Ted Thomasson," she clarified.

"And you are?" the reporter pressed.

"Caroline Lomax."

"Caroline," Ted snapped angrily, "don't give them our names."

"Oh." She swallowed quickly. "I didn't mean . . . Oh dear." She felt utterly and completely confused.

Without allowing her to speak further, Ted took her hand and led her away. Even as they briskly walked down the wide corridor, they were followed by the reporters, who hounded them with a series of rapid-fire questions.

To every one, Ted responded in a crisp voice, "No comment."

"What about you, Miss?"

Still reeling from the shock of the encounter outside the courtroom, she opened and closed her mouth, unsure what to say. A fiery glare from Ted convinced her to follow his lead. "No comment."

Because his stride was so much longer than her own, she was forced to trot to keep even with him. "Where are we going?" she asked breathlessly as they raced down the steps and sped toward the parking lot.

"I'm taking you home."

"Home," she echoed, disappointed. Tonight she would have enjoyed a leisurely drink or a peaceful dinner out.

He stopped in front of his car, took out his key and pressed the button to unlock the doors. Before he had a chance to open the passenger door for her, Caroline climbed inside. Ted stared at her for a long moment, then opened his own door and slid in. He braced his hands against the steering wheel and exhaled sharply. She understood his feelings. She had never been so glad to be out of a place in her life. Not even when she'd been caught raising prissy Jenny Wilson's gym shorts up the flagpole had she felt more glad to escape a situation. The leather-upholstered seat felt wonderful, almost comforting. The tension eased from her stiff limbs, and she slowly expelled a long sigh of relief as she leaned her head back. It felt like heaven to close her eyes.

Wordlessly, Ted started the engine and pulled out of the narrow space.

The silence was already grating on her as they pulled onto the busy Seattle street, which was snarled with rush-hour traffic. She searched her mind for something casual to say and came up blank. When she couldn't stand it any longer, she gave in and asked the question that had been paramount in her mind.

"Are you still angry with me?" she asked tentatively, surprised by how much the answer mattered to her.

"No."

"Good." For the life of her, she couldn't come up with something more clever to say. She was too drained emotionally to be original and come up with some witty remark that would restore the balance to their relationship. The funny part was that though she wasn't entirely sure they were capable of being friends, a whole day of hostility had left her decidedly upset. Previously, she'd delighted in tormenting him, had taken pride in coming up with ways to needle "Tedious Ted." Lately, though, she'd been hard-pressed to know who was tormenting whom.

Instead of pulling into the parking lot across the street from her apartment building, Ted eased to a stop at her curb.

"You aren't coming in?"

"No."

"Why not?" He made no move to

turn and look at her, which only served to upset her further.

"It's been a long day."

"It's barely four-thirty," she countered. In her mind she'd pictured spending a quiet evening together. She'd even thought of cooking a meal for him, so she could impress him with her considerable culinary skills. After a day like theirs, they needed to talk and unwind.

"Another time, maybe."

Just the nonchalant way he said it grated on Caroline's nerves. She knew a brush-off when she heard one. What did she care if he came inside or not? She wasn't desperate for a man's companionship. She didn't even like Theodore Thomasson, so it wasn't any skin off her nose if he preferred his own company. At least that was what she told herself as she swallowed back the unpleasant taste of disappointment.

"All right. I'll see you tomorrow, then," she said, tightening her hand around the door handle. Still she hesitated, not wanting to part. "Thanks for the ride."

"You're welcome."

If he didn't stop being so polite, she was going to scream. Finally she got out, and when she was safely on the sidewalk and had closed the car door, he pulled away. He didn't even have the common decency to speed. She would have liked him better if he had. For a long moment she didn't move. He might claim that he'd forgiven her, but she knew he hadn't. His sleek Chevrolet was long out of sight when she finally sighed with defeat and entered her apartment building.

As it turned out, she didn't even bother cooking a meal. After years of schooling to be a cordon bleu chef and countless arguments with her father over her chosen vocation, she ate a bowl of corn flakes in front of the television. The mistrial was barely given a mention on the local news, leaving her relieved. She felt as if she were wearing a scarlet letter as it was.

Tucking her bare feet beneath her, she leaned her head back and closed her eyes as a talk show came on after the national news. The next thing she knew, the sound of shrill ringing assaulted her ears, jolting her into full awareness. Straightening, she searched around her for the source. The phone pealed again, and she reached for it.

"Hello."

Hollow silence was followed by an irritating click.

Angrily, she stared at the receiver, silently accusing it of rousing her from a sound nap. A deep yawn shuddered through her, and she wrapped her sweater more tightly around her. She supposed she was glad Ted hadn't come inside after all. As sleepy as she was, she wouldn't have been much of a hostess. She told herself he had probably recognized how much the day had drained her, that he was only being thoughtful when he refused her invitation. She told herself that, but deep down she knew it wasn't true.

Although she'd had a long nap, she slept well that night and woke refreshed early the next morning. She dreaded another day at the court-house. There was a possibility she could be called to sit on another trial. The thought filled her with apprehension.

As she was grabbing her raincoat, the phone rang. She answered it on the second ring, and once again the caller immediately disconnected. Slowly Caroline replaced the receiver, perplexed.

Ted was already seated in the jury room when she arrived. She felt a sense of relief at seeing him and took the vacant chair next to him. He glanced up from his crossword puzzle but didn't greet her.

"Did you try to phone me last night?" she asked, sipping coffee from the steaming cup she'd picked up on her way in. It burned her mouth, and she grimaced.

"No." He gave her a look of condescension, as if to say she ought to know enough to let her coffee cool before trying to drink it. But that was the sensible thing to do, and she had never been sensible.

"What about this morning?" she asked.

"I didn't phone you this morning, either."

He didn't need to sound so pleased with himself. So he hadn't phoned. Deep down, she'd hoped it had been him.

"The reason I asked," she hurried to explain, "is that twice now someone has phoned and hung up when I answered. Caller ID just said private caller."

"Surely you don't think I —"

"No," she interrupted. "Listen, I'm sorry I asked. It was a mistake. Okay?" Irritated, she crossed her legs and studied his crossword puzzle, amazed that it was nearly complete. She hated the ones that gave the average solution time. It took her twenty minutes just to sharpen her pencil, find a comfortable position and figure out one-across. Since she was lousy at them, it naturally meant that Ted was a whiz at crossword puzzles. If the one he set aside now was any indication, he could win competitions.

The morning passed slowly. Several panels were called out for jury selection, but her name was not among them. That was more than fine with her.

At lunchtime Ted left the building without suggesting they eat together. She'd expected that, although she couldn't help feeling a twinge of regret. Without meaning to follow him, she discovered that they'd chosen the same place along the waterfront where they'd eaten a few days earlier. As usual, the outdoor restaurant was crowded, and once her order had been filled, there wasn't a place to sit. She could ask some strangers if they would mind sharing a table with her, but no one looked that interesting.

"Do you mind if I sit down?" she finally asked, standing directly in front of Ted.

"Go ahead." He didn't sound welcoming, but at least he didn't sound unwelcoming, either.

"I didn't follow you here," she announced, pulling out the bench opposite him. Vigorously she stirred her thick clam chowder.

"I didn't think for a minute that you had." He avoided her eyes and sat looking out over the greenish waters of Puget Sound.

"Are you always like this?"

"How do you mean?" He turned his gaze to her for an instant, then looked back to the choppy waters, seeming to prefer the view of the busy waterway to her.

"Are you always sullen and uncommunicative when you're angry with someone?" She considered it her greatest weakness that she really was miserable when someone was upset with her. In the past, this personality quirk had only applied to people she cared about, which meant that her current uneasiness over Ted was troubling her more every minute.

"Usually," he agreed.

"How long does it last?"

"That depends," he said, nibbling on a French fry.

"On what?"

"On how offended I am."

"How much have I offended you?"

"On a scale of one to ten," he stated casually, "I'd say a solid nine."

A thick lump worked its way down Caroline's dry throat. She had done some regrettable things in her life, and pulled enough shenanigans to cause her father a headful of gray hair. But there hadn't been a time when she regretted any words more than she regretted the ones she'd spoken to Ted. She'd felt recently that they had been on the brink of something special. She didn't know how to explain it. She wasn't even sure she liked him, but she felt a strange and powerful attraction to him. "I can't do anything more than apologize."

"I know." A sad smile touched the edges of his mouth. He didn't say anything when she slid off the bench and stood. She wanted to ask him how long he planned to be this way but didn't. They only had one more day of jury duty, and from the looks of things it would take far more time than that.

If the morning was dull, the afternoon was doubly so. Caroline intentionally sat as far away from Ted as possible, doing her best to ignore him. Yet again and again, as if by a force more potent than her own will, her gaze was drawn to him. He was by far the most attractive man in the room. There was a quiet authority about him that commanded the respect of others. The masterful thread in his voice hadn't gone unnoticed, either. From her experience being on the jury with him, she knew that he was quick, sure and decisive. If it hadn't been for his strength against the others, she sincerely doubted that she would have been able to withstand the concerted pressure to change her vote.

Later that afternoon she returned to her apartment, which didn't feel as welcoming as it usually did. Sluggishly she removed her backpack and looped it over the closest doorknob.

She was physically drained and mentally exhausted, and thoroughly disgusted with life. Once again her sense of timing had been off-kilter. She didn't know how to explain her life in better terms. It was as if everyone else was marching "left, right, left, right," and she was loping along her merry way — "right, left, right, left." Another woman would have looked at Ted Thomasson and immediately recognized what a devastatingly attractive man he was. She saw it, didn't trust it and chose to insult him. Only when it was too late did she recognize his appeal. At least after tomorrow their forced proximity would be over and she could go about her life, forgetting that she'd ever had anything to do with Tedious Ted Thomasson.

The phone started ringing at six that evening. The first time she was scrambling eggs for dinner and reached for it automatically. The pattern was the same. She picked up the phone, heard some distant breathing and then the caller disconnected. Obviously some weirdo had gotten her number and was determined to play games with her. Fifteen minutes later it happened again. After the third time, she unplugged her phone.

Refusing to give in to fear, she told herself that calls like these were normally harmless. What she needed to stir her blood was a little exercise. She changed into her jogging outfit and ran in place. She stopped only when the tenants below her began pounding on their ceiling. Panting, she turned off the record and slumped onto the sofa, panting.

Feeling invigorated and secure, she plugged her phone back in. It rang immediately. She practically jerked the receiver up to her ear. "If you don't stop bothering me, I'm calling the cops." That should frighten the jerk who was playing these games.

A moment of stunned silence followed. "Caroline, is that you?"

It was her mother.

"Oh, hi, Mom." She laughed in relief and briefly explained what had happened as she slumped against the thick sofa cushions. "I thought you were my prank caller."

"I'm so relieved," her mother said, and laughed softly. "You know how I live in fear of the police." Then she said, excitement brimming in her voice, "I have news. Your father and I are taking off for a little while." She paused, then added, "To China."

"China!"

"We leave tomorrow, and we're both very pleased. You know this is just the market he's been wanting to reach."

"How long will you be gone?"

"Two weeks. It's going to be a wonderful trip."

"It sounds like it." Caroline would miss her mother. Although they lived several hundred miles apart, they talked at least twice a week.

"Have you seen Theodore again?" The question had been asked casually, but she knew her mother well enough to sense the interest she was struggling to disguise.

"I see him every day in the jury room."

"He's grown up into someone pretty impressive, don't you think?"

"Yes, Mom, I do."

"You do?" Her mother was clearly having trouble disguising her surprise, and the line went silent for a moment. "You like him, don't you?"

"I insulted him. I didn't mean to, but it just slipped out, and now I doubt that we're capable of anything more than a polite greeting."

"He'll get over it," her mother said knowingly.

"Sure, just as soon as the moon turns blue."

"Caroline, I saw the way he looked at you. He'll come around, don't worry."

Caroline wished she had as much confidence as her mother, but she didn't.

■ ■ ■ ■

The next morning it was Caroline who arrived at the federal courthouse first. She'd brought along a book to occupy her time — a best-seller that was said to be irresistibly absorbing. She certainly hoped so.

When Ted entered the room, she pretended to be immersed in the thrilling plot of the book, though she couldn't even remember its title, let alone the characters or the story.

He took the seat beside her. "Morning." The greeting was clipped.

"Hello." She continued reading, proud that she'd resisted the urge to turn and smile at him, then cursed her heart for pounding because she was so glad he'd chosen to sit beside her.

"Did you try to phone me last night?" he questioned dryly.

So that was it. "No."

He leaned back in his chair and rubbed a hand over his face. "Someone was playing tricks on me half the night. Phoning, then hanging up."

"Surely you don't think I would do something like that?" She snapped her book closed and stiffened. "I'll have you know —"

"Caroline," he said, and gently placed a hand over hers to stop her. "Weren't you telling me the same thing was happening to you?"

"Yes," she said, still angry that he would think she'd done something so childish and trying not to remember that she'd all but accused him of the same thing just yesterday.

"Did it happen again last night?"

"Yes." She turned frightened eyes to him as she felt her facial muscles tense. "I thought it was a prankster . . . a joker, but now it's happening to you, too?"

"I don't think it's anything to worry about."

"Probably not," she agreed, but in truth she was frightened out of her wits. "But I think there has to be some connection between the phone calls and the trial."

"Still . . . a friend of mine is a detective. It might be a good idea if we have a chat with him."

"Do you think it's necessary?"

"I don't know, but I'd feel better if we knew where we stood."

"We're not standing anywhere. We're sitting ducks."

"Caroline, we're not. Whoever is

doing this is angry because of the mistrial, but it will blow over in a day or two." His face revealed none of his thoughts.

"Right," she said, crossing her legs and starting to nibble on her bottom lip. She wished he hadn't said anything about the calls he'd gotten. Ignorance really was bliss.

"Listen," he announced a minute later. "I'm sure I'm just overreacting. We've both gotten a few harmless phone calls, but there's no need to contact the police."

She wasn't nearly as convinced, but she let the subject drop.

They sat together for the rest of the day, though they barely spoke. At lunchtime they bought sandwiches and ate in the cafeteria.

"I'll drive you home," Ted announced at the end of the day.

Caroline didn't argue. Silently they walked toward the parking lot. Her hands were tucked deep within the pockets of her light jacket. She had a sinking feeling that something was about to happen, which caused chills to run up and down her spine. She would never lay claim to possessing any supernatural insight, not in the least, but her imagination had flipped into overdrive.

Ted stopped abruptly and released a mumbled curse.

"What's wrong?"

He pointed to his car, which had been smeared with raw eggs.

Caroline's earlier chill became so intense that she feared frostbite. "The person who did this has to be the same one who's making the phone calls," she murmured, struggling to disguise her alarm. If he was doing this to Ted, then something was bound to happen to her, as well.

"We don't have any proof of that."

He sounded so calm and reasonable that she wanted to shake him. "What are we going to do?"

"For starters, we'll head for a car wash."

"And then?"

"And then my friend's office."

"Okay." She was more than ready to agree.

Detective Charles Randolph was a brown-haired, clean-shaven man whose mouth widened with a ready smile when Ted walked into his office. Caroline followed closely on his heels and nodded politely when introduced. She resisted shaking hands, since hers were clammy with fear.

Ted briefly explained the reason for their visit. Detective Randolph sympathized, but he told them that chances were good their tormentor would stop his games in a day or so, and then he added that there was little he could do. He did offer some helpful suggestions, and assured them that the minute they could pinpoint a suspect or prove anything, he would do everything within the limits of the law to put an end to the problem.

Afterward Ted escorted Caroline to her apartment, and this time he accepted her invitation to go up for a cup of coffee. This time she ground the beans and went through elaborate steps to prolong the process to keep him with her as long as possible.

"You're not frightened, are you, Caroline?" he asked, his eyes dark and serious as he studied her.

"Who, me?" She laughed bravely and claimed the overstuffed chair across from him, her hands cupping her steaming mug.

"I agree with Randolph. Whoever is doing this is unlikely to hurt either one of us."

"Right." *Wrong,* her mind countered.

Ted didn't take more than a few sips of his coffee before he stood. Caroline sent him a pleading glance, but she wasn't about to ask him to stay if he was intent on leaving. She might be frightened half to death, but she still had her pride.

"Don't let any strangers into your

apartment," he cautioned.

Was he kidding? Her own brother would have to break down the door.

"Call me if anything happens. Okay?" he went on.

Wonderful. She had to wait until her life was in danger before contacting him. "Define 'happens.' " Her eyes were begging him to stay, to move in if necessary, at least until this craziness passed.

Ted appeared to be weighing her question. "You'll know."

"That's what I'm afraid of."

He hesitated in the open doorway. "You're sure you'll be all right?"

"I'll be fine." She was shocked that she could lie with such ease, but if he was determined to leave her to an unknown fate, then she would let him. No wonder she'd disliked him so much all these years. Maybe this was how he'd chosen to take his revenge.

He waited on the other side of the apartment door until she turned the lock and it clicked into place.

After he left, she managed to push the crank caller to the back of her mind by keeping busy. She baked bran muffins and ate one with a slice of bologna and cheese for dinner. Everything on television bored her, so she picked up the book she'd tried to read earlier that day with no success. By ten-thirty her eyelids were drooping. Chastising herself for being afraid to go to sleep, she slipped into her nightgown and started humming the national anthem. Her duty as a patriotic citizen had gotten her into this mess.

She crossed the room to pull the drapes closed when she noticed a burly figure of a man standing on the sidewalk below. He looked like the same man who had accompanied Joan MacIntosh. The resemblance was enough to cause her heart to flutter wildly and panic to fill her.

Ted had told her to wait until something happened. But she wasn't waiting until the commando below decided to break into her apartment.

Her fingers were shaking so badly that she could barely punch out Ted's telephone number.

He answered on the first ring.

"Ted." She heard the nervous tremor in her voice and tried unsuccessfully to calm herself.

"What is it?" He was instantly alert.

"A man . . . The man from the

trial . . . he's here."

"In your apartment?"

"Not yet. He's standing outside my building. I . . . went to close the drapes, and I saw him staring up at my window."

"Did he see you?"

"I don't know," she said sarcastically. "Do you want me to stick my head out the window and ask him?"

"Are you sure it's him? Nelson Bergstrom?"

"Not Nelson, Joan MacIntosh's husband. At least I think it's him. He was standing in the shadows, but it looked like it was him, and . . ."

"Caroline," he said her name so gently that she wanted to cry. "You're worrying too much. It's probably nothing."

"Nothing?" she echoed, hurt and

angry. "I'm locked in an apartment with a man seeking revenge outside my door. In the meantime you're probably sitting there in front of a cozy fireplace, smoking your pipe and . . . and you have the nerve to tell me I'm overreacting."

"Caroline —"

A loud knock sounded against her door and echoed like a taunt around the room.

"What was that?" Ted asked.

"He's here," she whispered, so frightened she thought she was going to faint.

FIVE

"Caroline!" Her name was followed by frantic pounding on her front door. "Caroline! Are you all right?"

"Ted?" His name was wrenched from the strangle-hold of shock and fear that gripped her throat. Her hands were trembling so hard that she could barely unlatch the door and open it. A shock wave shuddered through her bones at the sight of him. His eyes were narrowed and hard, and flickered possessively over her like tongues of fire, checking to see that she was unharmed. She had never seen a more intense expression. At that moment, she didn't doubt that he would have seriously hurt anyone who'd hurt her.

"Thank God." He closed the door and swept her into his arms, crushing her slender frame to his with such force that the oxygen was knocked from her lungs. She didn't care how hard he held her. He was here, and she was safe. She wanted to tell him everything that had happened, but the only sounds that escaped her fear-tightened throat were gibberish.

The unexpected strength of his kiss forced her head back so that she was pressed against the apartment wall. He moved his hands to cup her face, and his mouth pillaged hers with such hunger that her knees gave way. Her grip on his shoulders was the only thing that kept her upright. Consuming fear gave way to delicious excitement as she opened her mouth to him and met his lips with burning eagerness. His touch chased away the freezing cold of stark fear, and she nestled closer to his warmth, trembling violently. When his mouth trailed down her throat to explore her neck, Caroline fought her way through the haze of engulfing sensations. For days she'd wanted Ted to kiss her. She'd planned to treat him as he'd done her and make fun of him with some cutting remark. But one kiss and she'd melted into his arms. Her resistance amounted to little more than wafer-thin walls. Of course, the circumstances undoubtedly had something to do with the strength of her response. And now, instead of rejecting him, she held him as if she wasn't sure she could survive if he let her go.

"He didn't hurt you?"

"No." Her voice wavered, betraying the havoc he was causing to her self-control.

"When I saw the blood, I think I went a little crazy."

"Blood?" He wasn't making any sense. She hadn't answered the knock, and whoever wanted in had been content to make a few strange noises outside her door before leaving.

"The door," Ted muttered. His hands roved gently up and down her spine, molding her closer to him, as though he couldn't let her go.

"I didn't let him in." She still wasn't sure what he was talking about, but it didn't seem to matter when he was touching her with such tenderness.

"Caroline." He lifted his head long enough for the intimate look in his sapphire eyes to hold her captive.

"Yes?"

He shook his head from side to side, as if he couldn't bring himself to speak. Ever so slowly he lowered his mouth to hers again. She breathed deeply to control the excitement that tightened her stomach. If his first kiss had shocked her into melting bonelessly, this kiss completely and utterly devastated her.

Her hands strained against his shirt, clenching and bunching the material, but she didn't know if she meant to push him away or pull him closer. After a moment she didn't care.

"I would have hurt him — a lot —

if he'd touched you," Ted growled against her lips.

Remembering the feral light in his eyes earlier, she didn't doubt his words.

His breath filled her lungs. It felt warm and drugging, muddling her already-confused thoughts. "But he didn't, and I'm fine." Or she would be once her blood pressure dropped, but she didn't know who to blame for that — the lunatic or Ted.

Relaxing his hold, Ted slid his arm around her waist and securely locked the front door. "All right, my heart's back where it belongs. Tell me what happened."

His heart might have been fine, but hers wasn't. She felt as if she was standing on a dangerous precipice where the view was heavenly and heady, and stepping off looked like a distinct possibility. But she had only to look down the deep abyss below to realize what dangerous ground she was standing on. Mentally she took a step in retreat.

"Caroline," he coaxed, tenderly guiding her to the cushioned chair and sitting her down. He knelt in front of her, his hands clasping hers. "Tell me what happened. Tell me everything."

"Nothing happened, really. He — or whoever it was — knocked a few times. I . . . I didn't answer, and after a little while and a few weird noises, he went away." She didn't add that she'd stood stock-still, deathly afraid that whoever was doing this would come back. Not knowing if she should run from the apartment or stay put, she had waited, praying that Ted would arrive before her tormentor decided to return.

Ted expelled his breath. "I think I broke the land speed record getting here. If anything had happened to you, I never would have forgiven myself."

"I wouldn't have forgiven you, either," she said, rallying slightly, remembering how he'd abandoned her to an unknown fate earlier. "Why didn't you stay with me before? I was frightened and you knew it, yet you chose to leave."

"I couldn't stay." He raised his head, but he refused to meet her gaze. "I had another commitment."

"Another commitment." She spoke the words with all the venom of a woman scorned. So Theodore Thomasson had some hot date that was more important to him than her welfare. How incredibly stupid she'd been not to have guessed it sooner. No wonder he hadn't been able to get out of her apartment fast enough.

Raging to her feet, she stalked to the other side of the room as two bright spots of color blossomed in her cheeks. He'd left the arms of another woman to rescue her, then had the nerve to kiss her like that. She felt as if she was going to be sick. The worst part was that she'd kissed him back, encouraged him, and, yes, wanted him. Her throat ached as she battled back stinging tears.

"Well, as you can see, I'm unscathed." She did her best to sound normal. "Now that you've assured yourself of that, you'll want to go back to the ready arms of your calendar girl. I apologize if I inconvenienced your plans in any way."

"My calendar girl? What are you talking about?" he asked in confusion. "Have you taken leave of your senses?"

"Yes," she said. She had indeed abandoned sanity the minute he'd pulled her into his arms. "And don't you ever . . . ever —" She whirled on him, pointing her index finger at him like a weapon. "Don't you ever touch me again."

A weary glitter shone in his eyes, as if he were attempting to make sense of her words. "From the impression you gave me, I'd say you were enjoying my kiss."

"I was in shock," she countered, her expression schooled and brittle. "I didn't know what I was doing."

He ran his fingers through his hair, mussing it all the more. "All right, all right, we both didn't know what we were doing. Chalk it up to the unpleasant events of the last week. I'll admit kissing you was a mistake."

"I don't want it to happen again."

His frown deepened into a dark scowl. "It won't. Does that soothe your outrage?"

She swallowed past the lump that was choking her throat. Her answer was little more than a curt nod. "You can go now," she finally managed. She shivered, then wrapped her arms around herself to ward off the sudden chill. Ted opened her closet and took out a bulky-knit cardigan. It cost her more pride than he knew to let him drape it around her shoulders.

"Where's a bucket?" he asked, taking off his coat and rolling up his shirt sleeves.

"A bucket?"

"A couple of rags, too, if you have them?"

"Why?"

"Why?" he repeated, glancing at her as though she'd lost her mind. "Because of the blood."

Her face went sickly pale as she suddenly remembered what he'd said earlier. "What blood?"

"You didn't see your door?"

"No. What's wrong with it?" She marched across the room, but Ted stopped her before she made it halfway to the door. Their eyes locked in a battle of wills. "Ted?"

"There are a few unsavory words painted on it. I'm sure you've read them before."

"He — he wrote something on my door . . . in blood?"

"It's probably spray paint, but I thought . . . never mind what I was thinking."

"But . . ."

"Just get me a bucket, Caroline."

Numbly, she complied, leading the way into her kitchen and taking out a yellow plastic pail from beneath her sink. "Why would he knock if all he wanted to do was write some ugly words on my door? That doesn't make any sense."

"After spending this week in your company, there's little left in this world that does. How do I know what he was thinking? Maybe he wanted to know if you were home before he defaced your property," he said, and his mouth thinned with irritation. He took the plastic pail from her hands and filled it with soapy water. "And for that matter, who knows what he would have done if you *had* opened the door."

"There was no chance of my doing that. Maybe he would have gotten scared if I answered and gone away."

"There's no way of knowing that." Preoccupied, he pulled open a kitchen drawer and withdrew a couple of clean dishrags.

"There's no need for you to clean up. I'm perfectly capable of washing my own front door. Besides, you probably want to get back to your hot date."

"My hot date?"

"Would you stop repeating everything I say?"

His gaze seized hers in a hold that felt as physical and punishing as if he'd grabbed her arm. Pride demanded that she meet his eyes, but it wasn't easy. Never had Caroline seen anyone look so angry. His dark blue eyes were snapping with fire. "You certainly have a low opinion of me."

"I — You were the one who said you had an earlier commitment."

"And you assumed it was with a woman."

"Well . . . yes." She wished her voice would stop wavering. "You mean it wasn't?" Each word dropped in volume until they emerged in little more than a low whisper.

He didn't answer her. "Why don't you change your clothes while I wipe down your door?"

"Change my clothes?" For the first

time she realized that she was wearing a five-year-old flannel nightgown that had faded from a bright purple to a sick blue from years of washing. As if that wasn't bad enough, the hem had ripped out and was dragging against the floor. Complementing her outfit was a pair of glorious, scarlet knee-high socks.

"For once in your life, don't argue with me," he said in a voice that told her his patience was gone.

"I wasn't going to."

Ted's expression revealed surprise, but he said nothing more as he carried the yellow pail full of soapy water out her front door.

While he was about his task, Caroline changed into deep burgundy-colored cords and a fisherman's knit sweater. She knew that with her hair

she shouldn't wear colors like burgundy, but such taboos had always
been mere challenges to her. How
she wished she didn't have this pen-
chant for being so contrary.

Her hair was combed and tied at
the base of her neck with a pale blue
nylon scarf by the time Ted returned.
She followed him into the tiny
kitchen and watched as he emptied
the bucket, rinsed it out and placed
it back under the sink. When he
turned, he looked surprised to find
her close.

"You might want to pack a few
things."

"Pack a few things?"

"Now who's sounding like a par-
rot?"

In other circumstances she would
have laughed, but there wasn't any

humor in the look Ted was giving her.

"Why should I pack?"

"I'm taking you home with me."

"Why?" He made her sound like a puppy dog that needed a place to stay.

"Because I refuse to spend the rest of the night worrying about you." Each word was dripping with exasperation.

"It didn't seem to bother you earlier."

"It does now." Apparently that explanation was supposed to satisfy her. "Don't argue with me, Caroline. It won't do you any good."

From the scathing look he gave her, she could see that he was right. She could put up a valiant argument, but she was tired and afraid, and the truth was that she wanted to be with

Ted so much it actually hurt. The lunatic on her doorstep was only an excuse for enjoying his company. She'd been bitterly disappointed when Ted had left her earlier that evening. She'd longed to spend a quiet evening alone with him. There was a peacefulness about him that attracted her, an inner strength that drew her to him naturally. Yet all she'd managed to do was offend him. She reminded herself that he wasn't taking her to his apartment to enjoy her tantalizing company but out of a sense of duty. She swallowed her pride and followed him. She was going for more reasons than she cared to analyze.

Ted's apartment wasn't anything like what she'd imagined, though she *had* been right about the fireplace, which dominated the living room, with tan leather furniture positioned in front of it. Brass light fixtures were accentuated by the cream-colored carpet. Several paintings adorned the walls. Compared to her tiny apartment, Ted lived in the lap of luxury.

"I'll take your coat."

With a wan smile, she gave it to him. He'd barely spoken to her on the way over, and she once again sought for a way to tear down the concrete walls she'd erected between them with her thoughtless accusations. "Your apartment is very nice."

He looked as if he were about to answer her when the phone rang.

Her eyes widened with apprehension as he crossed the room. His back was to her, and although she couldn't hear much of the conversation, she saw Ted's shoulders sag in defeat. She had felt as if she'd been slowly crumpling under the oppressive weight of the pressure they'd been under these last few days, but Ted hadn't once revealed in any way that the trial and its outcome had affected him, so whatever was being said now must be far worse than anything they'd experienced so far.

Replacing the receiver, he turned to her. His eyes showed both anger and defeat.

"What is it?"

He rubbed his eyes and pinched the bridge of his nose. "That was Randolph."

"And . . . ?"

"He just wanted me to know that there's been another assault against a woman in a minimart."

"Nelson?"

"They don't know, but the MO's the same. Assuming our problems are tied to the trial, that can only inflame whoever's been harassing us, so he thinks it might be a good idea if we got out of town for a few days until the heat blows over."

Six

"Leave town? Whatever for?" Caroline watched with concern as Ted rubbed a hand across the back of his neck, looking as if the weight of the world were pressing against his shoulders.

"Don't you understand what I'm saying?" he barked. "Another young woman — a minimart clerk just like Joan MacIntosh — has been brutally assaulted. Pistol whipped in the same way as Joan, and from what Charles said, the cops are betting the same man who attacked Joan struck again tonight. And once again it was within walking distance of Nelson Bergstrom's address."

Caroline felt the strength leave her legs, and she slowly sank into a leather chair. Her voice wobbled as the tears that had hovered near the surface broke free. "And . . . and we set him free." Sniffling, she pressed her fingers to her eyes, but that did little good and the moisture ran unheeded down her ashen cheeks.

"We did what we thought was right," Ted countered. "We still don't know if Nelson Bergstrom is guilty or not. No one does."

"But it must've been him."

"Apparently the newspapers have gotten hold of this, and according to Randolph, the morning paper is doing a story about the mistrial in connection with this latest assault." He gave her his handkerchief and lowered himself into the chair beside hers. "Listen carefully, Caroline. The press have our names, and our addresses aren't exactly top-secret. They're going to have a field day with this, and we could be stuck in the middle of it."

"So we have to leave?"

"We don't *have* to, but Randolph advises it. I've been meaning to visit your parents anyway, and this seems like the perfect opportunity."

"We can't go see them. They've gone to China."

Ted nodded. "What about your brother?"

"No." She was just beginning to formulate her thoughts. She had a key to her parents' home. There wasn't any reason why she couldn't steal away there for a few days. "It shouldn't matter if Mom and Dad are gone. I'll take a couple of days and drive home, lounge around for a day or two, and head back. By then this thing will have been settled."

"You?" He gave her a disgruntled look. "We're in this together. Wherever *you* go, *I* go."

"You?" Caroline would have thought from the way he had been acting that the last person in the world he wanted to spend time with was her.

"Don't look so pleased," he murmured sarcastically, propelling himself out of the chair. "Believe me, I'm not all that thrilled to waste my time in *your* company, either."

"Then why do it?" she asked, feeling hurt and unreasonable. "I don't need you to escort me to San Francisco. I'm perfectly capable of taking care of myself."

"Listen, Miss High and Mighty, I had enough of you when I was fifteen to last any man a lifetime." He paused and pointed out the window. "But some loon is out there, seeking revenge because our actions set a guilty man free. You can bet that once this latest development hits the papers it's going to be more phone calls and messages smeared on doors — and maybe worse." His look cut right through her. "Now get this through that thick, stubborn skull of yours. I'm not sending you any place where I can't keep an eye on you. We're in this thing together, whether you like it or not."

Caroline had never seen Ted's eyes so flinty. Each word forced her deeper into the chair, until she felt as though she were physically embedded in the leather cushion. She crossed her arms in front of her in an attempt to ward off the hurt his words were inflicting, instead hugging the warm memory of his kiss to her heart. The burning heat from her cheeks dried her tears.

"Well?" he challenged, standing over her, apparently expecting an argument.

"When do you want to leave?"

Some of the diamond hardness left his eyes. "First thing in the morning."

"My clothes . . ."

"We'll pack tonight, catch what sleep we can, and leave first thing in the morning." He spoke impersonally, and Caroline had the impression that his thoughts were elsewhere. She could be a slab of marble for all the notice he gave her.

It took what felt like half the night to make the necessary preparations for the trip. Once she was packed and her apartment securely locked, they returned to his place. She offered to help and was refused without so much as a backward glance. When he went to get his things together, she sat on the sofa. She only meant to close her eyes and give them a rest, but the next thing she knew Ted was gently shaking her awake.

She sat up with a start. "What time is it?"

"Five-thirty. It might be a good idea if we left now."

"Okay." A headache was pounding at her temple, and she pressed her fingertips to it and inhaled deeply.

"There's coffee, if you'd like a cup."

She nodded, since conversation felt as if it would require a monumental effort. He stepped into the kitchen, then returned a moment later with a steaming mug. Her smile of appreciation drained her of strength, and she sagged back against the sofa cushions. He gazed at her, and she lowered her eyes, unwilling to let him see how miserable she felt. She could hear him moving around the apartment, and she took another sip of coffee, feeling the need for caffeine to inspire her to get moving.

"Here." Ted pried off the safety cap from a bottle of aspirin and shook two tablets into her palm.

"Thank you," she mumbled, accepting the glass of water he offered next. The tablets slid down the back of her throat easily. He had ranted at her earlier with an anger that had shocked her. Now he was tenderly seeing to her aches and pains. "Did you get any sleep at all?" she asked.

"No."

He didn't elaborate, but Caroline realized that, like her, he was feeling the heavy burden of responsibility for this latest assault case. Rationally, she recognized that they'd done what they felt was right by sticking to their convictions. But the fact they had felt the shadow of a doubt over Nelson Bergstrom's guilt didn't matter now. Every piece of evidence against the man had been circumstantial; they hadn't felt confident enough to hand over a guilty verdict. But this latest assault had jerked the rug out from under Caroline's feet. In her heart, she was sure that she had set a guilty man free.

"Did — did your friend at the police station mention how badly the latest victim was hurt? I mean . . ." She let the rest of the words fade, not wanting to know, yet realizing she must.

"She's in the hospital. Randolph said she's in pretty bad shape."

Caroline felt like weeping again, but she managed to hold back the tears with a suppressed shudder.

Twenty minutes later they were heading south on Interstate 5. Neither spoke and the air between them hung ominously heavy and still.

"How's the headache?" Ted asked as they approached the outskirts of the state capital in Olympia.

"Better." Her hand tightened on the

armrest of the car door. She doubted that the headache would go away until Nelson Bergstrom was in jail where he belonged — where she should have put him.

When Ted exited the freeway onto a secondary highway, she gave him a surprised glance. He answered her question before she voiced it.

"We're both drained. I thought we'd spend the day in Ocean Shores. I have a cabin there."

"That sounds like a good idea." She shifted to a more comfortable position in the seat, and his dark blue eyes slid briefly to her.

"When we get to the cabin we can catch up on some sleep, then leave again when it's dark and we won't be seen."

"Leave tonight? Why?" The idea of

spending a relaxing day on the beach was appealing to her. She needed the peace and solitude of a windswept shore to exorcize the events of the past week from her heart.

"I thought we should probably do our traveling by night," Ted explained. "It will be to our advantage to attract the least amount of attention possible."

Staring out the window at the lush green terrain, Caroline swallowed down a ready argument. The world outside the car window looked serene and peaceful, with its pastoral farms and grazing animals. The day was glorious, especially now in the light of early morning, as they raced down the highway with the rising sun that stood boldly out to greet them in hues of brilliant orange. She didn't want to argue with Ted, not now when she felt so tired and miserable. Telling him that he'd been watching too many cop shows wouldn't be conducive to an amicable journey.

More silence followed, but it wasn't harsh or grating; it was almost pleasant. Without being obvious, Caroline studied Ted. The image of him sitting in an office all day seemed strangely out of sync. His shoulders were too broad and muscular for a man who was tied to a desk. His jawline was solid, and there was a faint bend to his nose, as if it had been broken at one time. She couldn't picture him fighting, though she was sure he would if necessary. The last few days had taught her that. Another thing that amazed her was that he had never married. Fleetingly, she wondered why. He was more than attractive, compellingly male, and he stirred her blood as no one else ever had.

"You're looking thoughtful," Ted commented, his gaze momentarily turning toward her.

Caroline continued to study his handsome profile for a thoughtful second. "I was just wondering why you'd never married."

"No reason in particular." Amusement gleamed briefly in his eyes. "I've been too busy to settle down. To be honest, I've wondered the same thing about you."

"Me?" She half expected him to add a comment that she would be fortunate if any man wanted to put up with her. He had never seen the softly feminine part of her that yearned for a family of her own. No, he had only been witness to the shrewish part of her nature. "I've been too busy to think about a husband and home." The lie was only a small one.

"Your career is more important?"

Proving to her father that she could be the best cook in America had been more important. Her pride demanded it, but she couldn't tell Ted that. He would scoff and call her stubborn, and add a hundred other unsavory adjectives. And he would be right.

"Yes, I guess it is," she answered finally.

They didn't speak again until the road signs indicated that they were entering the community of Ocean Shores. Although she had heard a great deal about the resort town, with its rolling golf courses and luxurious summer homes, she had never been there. For herself, she would have chosen a less populated area, one with wide open spaces and room to breathe. She wouldn't want to worry about nosy neighbors or invading another's privacy. But her tastes weren't Ted's, and every minute together proved how little they shared in common.

When he turned off the main street and took a winding, narrow road that led down a secluded strip of wind-swept shore, then turned down his drive, Caroline was pleasantly sur-prised. His log cabin was far enough off the road so that it couldn't readily be seen.

He parked on the far side of the

house, so that his car wouldn't be easily visible from the road, either, and turned off the engine. He rested his hands on the steering wheel for a long moment as he closed his eyes.

"You must be exhausted."

They were less than three hours out of Seattle, but it felt as if they'd traveled nonstop to California.

"A little," was all he would admit.

The fireplace was the only source of heat inside the cabin, and Ted immediately started a fire. The place was small and homey, with only a few pieces of furniture.

Caroline looked around and came up with enough odds and ends from the kitchen cupboards to fix them something to eat. They were both hungry, and ate the soup and canned fruit as if it were ambrosia. While she washed and put away the few dishes they'd used, he sat on the sofa, staring into the fire, and promptly fell into a deep slumber. For a time she was content to watch him sleep. A pleasant warmth invaded her limbs, and she yearned to brush the hair from his brow and trace her hands over his strongly defined masculine features. Finding a spare blanket, she spread it over him, lingering at his side far longer than necessary.

A walk along the deserted beach lifted her heart from the doldrums and freed her eager spirit. Even when the sky darkened with a threatening squall, she continued her trek along the windy beach, picking up odds and ends of sea shells and bits of rock. The surf pounded relentlessly against the smooth beach. Crashing waves pummeled the sand until the undertow swept it away into the swirling depths. Caroline felt her own heart being lured into the abyss that only a few hours before had seemed so frightening. She was half a breath from falling in love with Ted Thomasson, and it frightened her to death.

Ted found her an hour later, building a sand castle with an elaborate moat and a bridge made from tiny sticks.

"I wondered where you'd gone," he said, and sat on a dried-out driftwood log. "You shouldn't have let me sleep so long."

"I figured you needed the rest." She glanced up into his warm gaze. Quickly she averted her eyes.

"We should be leaving soon."

"No." She shook her head for emphasis, her cloud of auburn curls twisted with the strength of her conviction.

"What do you mean — no?"

"I refuse to run away." She leaned back, sitting on her heels. Her hands rested on her knees as she met his puzzled gaze with unwavering resolve. "I realize that I've probably had a lot more experience in dealing with guilt than you have, and the first thing I've learned is —"

"Caroline —"

"No, please listen to me. We — *I* — did what I felt was right even when the decision wasn't easy. I refuse to punish myself now because I may have made the wrong choice. If there's someone out there who wants me to suffer because of that, then I'd prefer to meet him head-on rather than sneak around in the dark of night like a common thief. I simply won't do it."

The expression that crossed his face was so like her father's when she'd utterly exasperated him that Caroline suppressed the urge to laugh.

"You know I won't leave you," Ted admitted slowly.

"I'm hoping you won't, but I wouldn't stop you," she said, feeling brave. She hadn't planned on him driving off without her — she hadn't seen the necessity. He was much too much of a gentleman.

"It would be a simple thing for anyone looking for us to learn about this cabin. Our coming here makes sense."

"Don't worry, I've got that all figured out. We'll sleep on the beach tonight."

"We'll do *what?*" he exploded. "It's cold out here."

Caroline did an admirable job of holding back her laugh of pure delight. In the last twenty hours Ted had taken great pains not to touch her. Of course, she'd asked him not to, but that shouldn't matter. If they pitched a makeshift tent here on the sandy beach, he would be forced to seek her body's warmth. Although he would have every intention of avoiding it, he would wake up holding her in his arms. The mental image was one of such delight that she experienced a tingling warmth up and down her arms.

"I'll keep you warm," she promised under her breath, smiling.

He wasn't pleased with the rest of

her ideas, either, so she was astonished that he did as she asked. For dinner they roasted hot dogs on sticks and melted chocolate bars over graham crackers. By the time they'd eaten their fill, the first stars were twinkling in the purpling sky.

"I thought it might rain earlier this afternoon," she mentioned conversationally.

"If it did, maybe you'd listen to reason."

"Maybe," she said with a gleeful smile. "But I doubt it. I've always loved the ocean."

"It's cold and windy, and it's only a matter of time before everything smells like mold," Ted grumbled, tossing another dried piece of wood on the fire.

"Yet you bought a place by the

beach, so you must not dislike it half as much as you claim."

His answer was a soft snort as he wrapped a blanket more securely around his shoulders. "I don't need to worry about anyone hunting me down. One night with you and I'll be dead from pneumonia."

"Stop complaining and look at how beautiful the sky is."

"Bah humbug!" He rubbed his hands together and stuck them out in front of the sputtering fire.

The pitch-black night darkened the ocean, while the silvery beams of a full moon created a dancing light on the surface of the water.

"When I was a little girl I ran away to the sea. I was utterly astonished when they told me I couldn't board the ship."

Ted chuckled. "I remember my parents telling me about that. How old were you? Ten?"

"About that. I'd pulled one of my usual shenanigans — I can't even remember what it was anymore — but I knew that once again I'd embarrassed my mom and dad, so I decided to go to sea. I'll never forget when they came down to the docks to pick me up. My mother burst into tears and hugged me close. For the first time in my life, I realized how much she loved me."

"Had you doubted it before?"

"No, I'd simply never thought about it. No matter how I tried, I could never do things right. There would always be one reason or another why my marvelous schemes failed and I ended up with egg on my face. When I ran away I thought it was for the best, so I wouldn't embarrass Mom again. That night I learned that it didn't matter how many escapades I got myself into, she would always love me. I was her daughter."

"Did you ever try running away again?"

"Never. There wasn't any need. My home was with her and Dad." She centered her concentration on the bark she was peeling from an old stick. She didn't often speak of her youth, chagrined by her behavior.

"You were marvelous, Caroline Lomax. Full of imagination and sass. Your parents had every reason to be proud of you." He spoke with such insight that she raised her head, and their gazes met over the flickering fire. The mesmerizing quality in his eyes stole her breath. Her heart pounded so loud and strong that she was convinced he could hear it over the crashing of the ocean waves. When his attention slid to her softly parted lips, she was certain he was going to reach for her and kiss her. She held her breath in helpless anticipation, yearning for his touch.

Abruptly, he stood and tossed the blanket to the sandy ground. "I've had enough of this wienie roast. You can sleep out here if you want, but I'm going inside."

She tried to hide her disappointment behind a taunting laugh. "You always were a quitter."

He ignored her derision and shook his head. "I don't have your sense of adventure. I never did."

"That's all right," she mumbled,

standing. She brushed the sand from the back of her legs. "Few men do."

"You're coming with me?" He looked stunned that she'd conceded so easily.

"I might as well," she grumbled, mostly to herself. Ted helped her put out the fire, and haul the blankets and leftover food back to the cabin.

If she was disgruntled with his lack of adventure, the sleeping arrangements irritated her even more. "You go ahead and take the bed." He pointed to the bedroom, and the lone double bed with the thick down comforter and two huge pillows.

She had to admit it looked inviting. "What about you?"

"Me?" His Adam's apple worked as he swallowed convulsively. "I'll sleep out here, of course."

"But why?"

"Why? Caroline, for heaven's sake think about it."

"You can sleep on top of the covers if it will soothe your sense of propriety. I read once that if we each keep one foot on the ground, it's perfectly fine for two unmarried people to sleep in the same bed."

Clearly flustered, he waved his hand toward the bedroom. "You go on. I slept most of the day. I'm not tired."

A smile curved Caroline's full lips. She was enjoying riling him and, true to form, Ted was easy to rile. "I trust you."

"Maybe you shouldn't," he barked, and rubbed the back of his neck in a nervous gesture. "I can't believe you'd even suggest such a thing."

"Why? It only makes sense to share,

since there's only one bed."

"Good night, Caroline." He crossed his arms, indicating that the discussion was closed, and turned his back to her, standing stiffly in front of the fireplace.

"Good night," she echoed, battling to disguise her amusement.

She had no trouble falling asleep. The bed was warm and comfortable, and after only a few hours' sleep the night before, she slipped easily into an untroubled slumber.

Ted woke her at dawn and brought her in a cup of coffee. "Morning, bright eyes."

"Is it morning already?" she grumbled, yawning. Propping herself up on an elbow, she brushed the hair off her forehead. "How'd you sleep?"

"Great. You were right. Spending

the night on the sofa was silly when there was a comfortable bed and a warm body eager for my presence."

She bolted upright. "You slept in this bed?"

"You're the one who suggested it."

"Here? In this bed?" she said again, too amazed to come up with anything else.

"Is there another one I don't know about?"

"You didn't really!"

"Of course I did. Honestly, Caroline, have you ever known me to tease?"

She hadn't. Her mouth dropped open, but a shocked silence followed. For the first time in recent history, she was stunned into speechlessness.

"I'd like to leave in twenty minutes," he said, and set the steaming coffee mug on the dresser top. "Will that be a problem?"

She answered with a shake of her head, still not quite believing his claim about sleeping with her. Mystified, she watched him leave the room and gently close the door, offering her privacy.

Biting her bottom lip, she cocked her head as an incredulous smile touched her eyes. Faint dimples formed at the corners of her mouth. Maybe this trip wouldn't be such a disaster. It could turn out to be the most glorious adventure of her life. Even now, she had trouble believing that she found Ted Thomasson so appealing. Would wonders ever cease? She certainly hoped not.

Oregon's coastal Highway 101 stretched along four hundred miles of spectacular open coastline. With her love of the ocean, Caroline had made several weekend jaunts to the area. She never tired of walking the miles of smooth beaches, clam digging, beachcombing and doing nothing but admiring the breathtaking beauty of the unspoiled scenery.

"We'll need to stop in Seaside," she informed him once they crossed the Columbia River at Astoria.

"Why Seaside?"

"Historians agree that the Lewis and Clark trail ended on the beaches there."

"I don't need a history lesson. Unless it's important, I think we should press on."

From the minute they'd left the beach house that morning, he had seemed intent on making this trip a marathon undertaking. He didn't want to travel the freeway, and, to be honest, she was pleased. The coastline made for far more fascinating travel, and she had several favorite spots along the way.

"It's not an earth-shattering reason," she concluded, disappointment coating her tongue. "But Seaside has wonderful saltwater taffy, and I'd like to get a box for my mother. Taffy's her favorite, and she likes Seaside's the best, so —"

"All right. We'll make a quick stop," he agreed.

"Thanks." Sighing, she smoothed her palms down the front of her dark raspberry shorts. She couldn't understand Ted. His moods kept swinging back and forth. Last night he'd been good-natured and patient. This morning he was behaving as if they were fleeing a Mafia gang hot on their tail.

When they reached Seaside, he parked along the beachside promenade and cut the engine. "I'll wait here."

"In the car?" she asked disbelievingly. "But it's a gorgeous day. I thought you'd like to get something to eat and walk along the beach."

"I'm not hungry."

Glaring at him, she climbed out of the car and closed the door with unnecessary force. Maybe *he* wasn't hungry, but *she* was. They'd stopped for coffee and doughnuts at a gas station hours earlier, and that hadn't been enough to keep her happy. Fine! He could sit in the car if he liked, but she wasn't going to let his foul mood ruin her day. Every stride filled with purpose, she walked to the end of the street near the turnaround and bought a large box of candy for her mother. A vendor was selling popcorn, and she purchased a bag and carried it down the cement stairs to the sandy beach below.

Ted found her fifteen minutes later, sitting on a log and munching on her unconventional meal. "I've been looking all over for you," he said accusingly.

"Sorry." She offered some popcorn in appeasement, but she had no real regrets. "I got carried away. It really is lovely here, isn't it?"

"Yes." But he sounded preoccupied and impatient. "Are you ready to leave now?"

"I suppose."

Back on the highway, he turned and gave her a disgruntled look. "Is there any other place you'd like to stop?"

"Yes — two. Cannon Beach and Tillamook."

"Caroline, this isn't a stroll down memory lane. You must have seen these sights a hundred times. We're in a hurry. There's —"

"Correction," she interrupted briskly. "*You* appear to be in a rush here, not me. I explained once before that I refuse to run away. You can let me off at the next town if you insist on acting like this."

His hands tightened around the wheel until she was surprised he didn't bend it. "All right, we can stop in Cannon Beach and Tillamook, but what's there that's so all fired important?"

"You just wait and see," she said, feeling much better.

Less than a half hour later he pulled into a public parking area near Cannon Beach. While he grumbled and complained under his breath, she found a vendor and bought a huge box kite. Tight-lipped, he helped her assemble it, but then he only sat on the bulkhead while she raced up and down the shore, flying the oblong contraption. The wind caught her laughter, and she was breathless and giddy by the time she returned.

Ted gave her a sullen look and carted the kite to the car, setting it in the backseat next to the box of salt-water taffy.

Caroline wiped the wet sand from her bare feet before joining him in the front seat. Snapping the seat belt into place, she closed her eyes and made a gallant effort to control her tongue but lost. "You know, you're about as much fun as a bad case of chicken pox."

"I could say the same thing about you."

"Me?" she gasped, outraged. She was shocked at how much those words hurt. She swallowed back the pain, crossed her arms and stared straight ahead.

He started the engine and backed out of the parking space. The tension was so thick in the close confines of the car that it resembled a heavy London fog.

Thirty-five minutes later Ted announced that they were in Tillamook. She had been so caught up in her hurt and anger that she hadn't realized they were even close to Oregon's leading dairy land.

She pointed out the huge building to the left of the road. "I want to stop at the cheese factory," she said, doing her best to keep her voice monotone. She didn't bother to explain that her father loved Tillamook's mild cheddar cheese and she was planning on bringing him a five-pound block.

Ted sat in the car while she made a quick stop in the factory's visitor shop. He climbed out of the front seat when he saw her approach. She made only a pretense of meeting his cool gaze.

"Would you open the trunk, please?" she asked with a saccharine smile.

When he did, she lifted her heavy suitcase from inside and set it on the ground.

"What are you doing?" he demanded.

"What I should have done in the beginning." She opened the car door and took out the box of saltwater taffy and the kite, and sat them on the ground beside her suitcase. "This isn't working," she replied miserably. "It was a mistake to think the two of us could get along for more than a few hours, let alone a week."

He raked his hand through his hair. "Just what do you intend to do?"

She lifted one shoulder in a delicate shrug, hoping to give the impression of utter nonchalance. "The Greyhound bus comes through town. I'll catch that."

"Don't be ridiculous."

"I thought you'd be pleased to be

rid of me," she countered smoothly. "From the minute we left Ocean Shores this morning, you've been treating me like I was a troublesome pest. Here's your chance to be free. I'd take it if I were you."

"Caroline, listen. . . ."

"Believe me, I know when I'm not wanted." She'd suffered enough rejection when she was young to know the feeling intimately.

"I should have told you earlier," he said with gruff insistence, "but I didn't want to frighten you."

"I told you before, I don't scare easily."

"Do you remember when I gassed up the car this morning?"

She nodded.

"I phoned Randolph, and . . ." He paused, his look dark and serious.

"There's no easy way to say this. Apparently there's been a death threat made against us."

Seven

"A death threat." The ugly words hung in the air between them for tortuous seconds. "Who?"

"They don't know."

"So the threat wasn't phoned into the police station? Because they could have traced it then, right? So . . . how — how did Randolph hear about it?" In spite of her calm voice, her heart was pounding so hard she thought it might burst right out of her chest.

"Apparently someone wrote on the walls outside my apartment, as well.

This time the message was more than a few distasteful names. The neighbors phoned the police after an article came out in the morning paper."

"Your name was in the paper?" Caroline breathed in sharply and briefly closed her eyes.

"It turns out this is the seventh robbery of a minimart in which the cashier was pistol whipped. The MO's are identical in each case. The paper interviewed Nelson Bergstrom's arresting officer, and followed his case through the trial and what's happened since. The two of us aren't exactly going to be asked to run for the Seattle city council, if you get the picture."

Caroline did, in living color. "I see," she murmured, and swallowed at the lump thickening in her throat. An unexpected chill raced up her spine. "But surely whoever did this wouldn't follow us. . . ."

"No one knows what they're capable of doing." Ted rubbed his face, as if to erase the tension lines etched so prominently around his eyes and nose. "Randolph suggested that we stay clear of your parents' place in San Francisco, as well."

She agreed with a quick nod. "Then where do you think we'll be safe?"

"Brookings. Randolph has some connections there. He's making arrangements for us to rent a secluded cottage. That way he'll know where he can reach us."

No wonder Ted had been so disagreeable all morning. Numbly, she responded, refusing to allow fear to get the best of her, "That sounds reasonable."

His rugged features hardened into glacier ice. "I'm not letting you out of my sight anymore, Caroline, not for a minute. Do you understand?" His cutting gaze fell to her suitcase.

"I wish you'd said something before now. I thought you were sick of my company."

"Never that, sweetheart, never that." He used the affectionate nickname as if it had slid off his tongue a thousand times. Then, with deliberate, controlled movements, he lifted her suitcase and placed it back inside the trunk.

"Ted?"

He turned toward her, the hard mask of his face discouraging argument. "Yes?"

"Would you . . . mind holding me

for a minute?" For all her brave talk about refusing to run away, she was scared. Her blood was cold, and she felt weak with fright. People had disliked her over the years, but never enough to want to kill her.

Ted wrapped his arms around her and gathered her close. The warmth from his hard body warded off the icy chill that had invaded her limbs. She relaxed against him, letting her soft curves mold to the masculine contour of his body. She felt his rough kiss against her hair, the even rhythm of his pulse, and a soothing peace permeated her heart.

"Nothing's going to happen to you." His whispered promise felt warm and velvety, like a security blanket being draped around her. "Whoever comes after you will have to get through me first."

Scalding tears burned the backs of her eyes. For years she'd treated Ted Thomasson abominably. When they were younger, she'd teased him unmercifully, to the point of being cruel. Even as an adult and with the best of intentions, she'd managed to outrage him. Yet he was willing to protect her to the point of risking his own safety. She had never felt more humbled or more grateful. Frantically, she searched for the words to express her feelings, but nothing she could think of seemed appropriate.

"Would you like some cheese?"

"Pardon?" He relaxed his hold and lifted her chin so their gazes met.

"Mild cheddar," she said, and sniffled, though she managed to hold all but a few emotional tears at bay.

"I . . . I thought you might like some cheese."

"Another time. Okay?"

"Sure." She wiped the dampness from her cheek with the back of her hand and quickly redeposited her accumulated items inside the car.

Silence reigned as they took up their journey. Finally he reached for her hand and squeezed it reassuringly. "I should have told you sooner."

"I shouldn't have been so self-centered. Something was clearly troubling you. I was the one at fault for being so oblivious."

"Don't be ridiculous."

"Oh, Ted, how can you say that? I bought the kite just to spite you. I don't deserve anyone as good as you in my life and you certainly rate someone better than a troublemaker like me."

"Maybe, but I doubt it," he answered cryptically.

Before this latest stop she had felt his urgency and resented it. Now the need for haste was in her blood, as well. They barely spoke after that, both of them wrapped up in the troubles of the moment. Brookings represented safety; there were people there who would help them, people who were in contact with Detective Randolph in Seattle.

"Are you hungry?" Ted asked as they approached the outskirts of Lincoln City.

Caroline was convinced he'd asked because her stomach had been rumbling, but the pangs weren't from hunger. She glanced at him consideringly. Although she'd eaten the bag of popcorn, he hadn't had anything today except coffee and a sugar-coated doughnut. A look at her watch confirmed that it was after noon.

"Maybe we should stop."

"Anyplace special?"

"No," she said, "you choose." Lincoln City was a seven-mile-long community, the consolidation of five former small cities, with a wide assortment of restaurants and hotels. Caroline had visited there often on her way to San Francisco and enjoyed the many attractions.

Ted parked in the center of the town. Eager to stretch her legs, she stepped out of the car and lifted her arms high above her head as she gave a wide yawn.

"Tired?" he inquired, and smiled lazily.

"No," she assured him. "I'm just a little stiff from sitting so long." As she spoke, a German Shepherd approached her, his tail wagging eagerly. "Hello, big guy," she greeted him, stooping to pet his thick fur, which was matted and unkempt. "What's the matter, boy, are you lost?" The dog regarded her with doleful dark eyes. "He's starving," she announced with concern to Ted, who had walked around the car to join her.

"He probably smelled the cheese." Absently, he patted the friendly dog on the top of the head. "There's a good restaurant around the corner from here, as I recall."

"What about the dog?" she asked, slightly piqued by his indifference to the plight of the lost animal.

"What about him?"

"He's hungry."

"So am I. If he's lost, the authorities will pick him up sooner or later." A hand at her elbow led her toward the restaurant.

She resisted, shrugging her arm free. "You're honestly going to leave him here?" She twisted around to discover the dog seeking a handout from another passerby.

"I don't see much choice. A stray dog is not our responsibility."

From his crisp tone, Caroline could tell the discussion was closed. Her mind crowded with arguments. But he was right, and she knew it. Nonetheless, there had been something so sad in those dark eyes that it had touched her, and she couldn't put the pitiful dog out of her mind.

Even after they'd eaten and were lingering over their coffee, she continued to think about the lost dog. Neither of them spoke much, but the silence was companionable. When Ted stood to pay the cashier, she placed a hand on his arm and murmured, "I'll be right out front."

As she'd suspected, the German Shepherd was outside the restaurant, glancing hopefully at each face that walked out the door.

"I bet the smells from here are driving you crazy, aren't they, fellow?" She took a few scraps she'd managed to smuggle into a napkin without Ted noticing and gave them to the dog. He gobbled them down immediately and looked at her for more.

"How long has it been since you

ate?" The poor dog was so thin his ribs showed. Glancing around her, she spied a food vendor down the street. "Come on, boy, we'll get you something more."

The dog trotted at her side as she hurried down the block, past Ted's parked car and toward the beach. She bought four hot dogs and found a sandy spot off the side street to feed the starving dog.

After he'd eaten his fill, she regarded the sad condition of his fur. "You're a mess, you know that? What you need is a decent bath. Someone needs to comb your fur."

A flicker from those dark eyes seemed to say that he agreed with her.

"Caroline."

Her name was spoken with such

anger that she whirled around.

In her concern for the dog, she'd forgotten about Ted, and he was clearly furious. She forced herself to smile, but her heart sank to the pit of her stomach at the angry twist of his features. She hadn't meant to wander off, but she'd been so busy trying to take care of the dog that she had forgotten he didn't know where she'd gone.

"Just what do you think you're doing? You said you'd be right outside."

Responding to Ted's anger, the dog moved to Caroline's side and took up a protective stance, emitting a low growl.

"It's all right, boy. That's Ted." Caroline gave the dog a reassuring pat on the head.

"I should have known that animal

was somehow involved in this," Ted snarled. "Right out front, you said. Can you imagine what I thought when you weren't there? I swear, Caroline, my heart can't take much more of this. What do I have to do? Handcuff you to my side?"

"I'm sorry . . . honestly, I didn't mean to take off, but I couldn't stop thinking about the dog and —"

"Just get in the car. I'll feel a whole lot better once we're in Brookings."

"But . . ."

"Are we going to argue about that as well?"

She didn't want any more dissension between them. "No."

"Thank you for that." He turned and headed toward the car with a step that was as crisp as a drill sergeant's.

Gently patting the side of her leg to urge the dog to follow her, Caroline followed in Ted's wake. The German Shepherd didn't need any urging and trotted along happily at her side as if he'd been doing so all his life.

When she started to open the rear door, Ted cast her a scathing look. "Now what are you doing?"

"I — I was thinking that it might not be a bad idea to take the dog with us. He's hungry and needs a home. And I bet he'd offer us a lot of protection. I'm going to name him Stranger because —"

"We're not taking that filthy dog!" Ted exploded.

"But —"

"You've already managed to accumulate a box of candy, a slab of cheese and a sackful of worthless sea shells, in addition to a man-size kite. I absolutely refuse to take that dog. The answer is no. N. O. No."

Caroline turned away. "I get the picture," she replied tightly. She crouched down on one knee. "Good-bye, Stranger," she whispered to the dog. "I did the best I could for you. You take care of yourself. Someone else will come along soon — I hope."

The car's engine roared to life, and she swallowed down the huge lump in her throat before climbing in beside Ted, who sat still and unyielding, arms outstretched, gripping the steering wheel. She closed her eyes, biting back the words to ask him to reconsider. It wouldn't do any good; his mind was made up.

"Next stop is Brookings," he said as he checked the rearview mirror and pulled out of the parking space.

"Right," she agreed weakly.

Turning the corner, they merged with the highway traffic as it sped through town. Not wanting Ted to see the emotion that was choking her, Caroline turned and stared out the side window. A flash of brown and black captured her attention from the side mirror. Stranger was running for all his worth, following them down the highway. Cars were weaving around him, and horns were blaring.

"Stranger!" she cried, twisting around despite the seatbelt, so she was kneeling in the front seat and staring out the rear window. She cupped one hand over her mouth in horror as she watched the dog, his tongue lolling from the side of his mouth, persistently running, unaware of the danger.

"All right. All right." With a mumbled curse, Ted pulled over to the side of the road. "You win. We can take that stupid dog. Heaven only knows what else you're going to pick up along the way. Maybe I should rent a trailer."

The sarcasm was lost on Caroline, who threw open the car door and leaped out with an agility she hasn't known she possessed.

As if he'd been born to it, Stranger leaped into the open backseat of the car, curled into a compact ball and rested his chin on his paws. Still panting from exertion, he looked up at her with grateful eyes. She sniffled, and ruffled his ears before closing the back door and slipping in beside Ted.

"Thank you," she whispered brokenly to him. "You won't regret it, I promise."

"That is something I sincerely doubt."

The tires spun as he pulled the car pulled back onto the highway. Having gotten her way when she'd least expected it, she tried her best to be pleasant company, chatting easily as they continued south.

He made a few comments now and again, but his lack of attention irritated her. The least he could do was pretend that he was interested.

"Am I boring you?" she asked an hour later.

"What makes you think that? I'm thrilled to know the secret ingredient in bran muffins isn't the bran." His well-defined mouth edged up at one corner in a mirthless grin that bordered on sarcasm.

Fuming, she crossed her arms over her breasts and focused her gaze straight ahead. Ted wasn't pleased about the dog, but he didn't need to pout to tell her that. For that matter, she wasn't exactly sure what *she* was going to do with Stranger, either. But leaving him behind to face an uncertain fate was an intolerable thought. She simply couldn't do it. To be truthful, she had been shocked that he had been so heartlessly willing to leave the dog behind, though he'd redeemed himself by pulling over and letting Stranger in the car. In her own way, she'd been trying to tell him that by being chatty, witty and pleasant. She was tired of arguing with him. She wanted them to be friends. Good friends. "I won't bother you anymore," she grumbled, swallowing her considerable pride.

Ted's gaze didn't deviate from the road, and his quiet low-pitched voice could barely be heard over the hum of the engine. "Not bother me? You've been nothing but trouble from the time we met."

She forced herself to relax against the seat, refusing to trade insults with him, though the words burned on her lips to tell him that he'd been easy to terrorize. That gentlemanly streak of his was so wide it looked like a racing stripe down the middle of his back.

"Has anyone ever commented on how your eyes snap when you're angry?" he inquired smoothly ten minutes later.

"Never."

"They do — and very prettily, I might add."

"You should be in a position to know."

He chuckled and turned on the radio. Apparently listening to the farm report was more interesting than her attempts at conversation had been.

They stopped for gas in Florence, outside of Dunes City. Had things been more amiable between them, she might have suggested that they stop and explore the white sand aboard rented camels. It had always been her intention to hire a dune buggy and venture into the forty-two-mile stretch of sand, but she never had. The camels were a new addition, and she would have loved to ride one. Knowing Ted's preferences, he would have chosen to stand at the lookout point, utterly content to snap pictures.

Thinking the situation over, it shocked her once again to realize how different she was from this man. Even more jarring was the knowledge that it would be so easy to fall in love with him.

"I might have been tempted to stop here and take a few pictures," he confessed, echoing her thoughts, "but I don't think the car is big enough to hold both a camel and a dog." Amusement gleamed in his eyes, and she chuckled, appeased by his wit. He was full of surprises. Until recently, she had thought the highlight of his week was breaking in a new pair of socks. Now she was learning that he had wit and charm, and she had to admit, she enjoyed being with him when he was like this.

They drove for what seemed an eternity. She couldn't recall ever being so comfortable with silence. He was content to listen to the radio. Stranger, who had slept for most of the journey, now seemed eager to arrive at their destination. He sat up in the backseat and rested his paw beside her headrest.

The car's headlights sliced through the semidarkness of twilight, silhouetting the large offshore monoliths against the setting sun. The beauty of the scene was powerful enough to steal Caroline's breath.

"It's lovely, isn't it?" she murmured, forgetting the reason for this exile.

"Yes, it is," he agreed softly. "Very beautiful."

Briefly, their eyes met, and he offered her a warm smile that erased a lifetime of uncomplimentary thoughts.

"We'll be there soon."

She responded with a short nod. The quiet felt gentle. She could think of no other word to describe it. A tenderness was growing between them. They'd both fought it, neither wanting it, yet now they seemed equally unwilling to destroy the moment.

"Caroline," he finally murmured, then paused to clear his throat.

"Hmm?"

"There's something I should tell you now that we're near Brookings."

"Yes?"

Whatever he had to say was clearly making him uneasy. He studied the road as if they were in imminent danger of slipping over the edge and crashing to the rocks below.

"This morning, when I talked with Randolph . . ." He hesitated for a second time. "I want you to know that he was the one who suggested this."

"Suggested what?" She studied him with renewed interest. The pinched lines around his mouth and nose didn't speak of anger as much as uneasiness.

He ran a hand along the back of his neck and expelled his breath in a low groan. "What I'm about to tell you."

"For crying out loud, would you spit it out?"

"All right," he snapped.

Stranger, apparently sensing the tension, barked loudly.

"Tell that stupid dog to shut up."

"Stranger is not stupid." Twisting around, Caroline scratched the German Shepherd behind the ears in an effort to minimize the insult. "He didn't mean that, boy," she whispered soothingly.

"Caroline, listen, what I'm about to tell you is none of my doing. Randolph seemed to feel it was necessary."

"You've said that twice. Would you kindly quit hedging and tell me what's going on?"

"We're going to have to pose as a newlywed couple."

"What?" she exploded, stunned.

"Apparently the people who own the cottage are old fashioned about this sort of thing, but it's safest if we stay together, so Randolph suggested the newlywed thing. I don't like it any better than you do."

A bemused smile blossomed on her lips. "Does this mean I'm going to have to bat my eyelashes at you and fawn over your every word?" She couldn't help giggling. "Will I need to pretend to be madly in love with you?" She was afraid that wouldn't call for much acting on her part.

"No," he returned sharply. "It just means we're scheduled to share a cottage."

"Oh, good grief. Is that all?"

Ted glanced at her sharply. "Well, doesn't that bother you?"

"Should it?"

"You're behaving as though you do this sort of thing often."

She decided to ignore the censure in his voice. "I don't see much difference between sharing a honeymoon cottage and spending the night in your one-bed cabin."

"Well, you needn't worry, I'll sleep on the couch."

"Now that's ridiculous. I'm a good six inches shorter than you. If anyone sleeps on the couch, it'll be me."

"Can we argue about that later?"

Caroline released an exaggerated sigh. "I suppose."

Ten miles later she couldn't stay quiet a moment longer. "You know what's really bothering you, don't you?" There was no holding back her lazy smile.

"I have the feeling you're going to tell me." The sarcasm was back, although he tried to give an impression of indifference.

Reading him had always been so

easy for her. She wondered if others could decipher him as well as she could, then doubted it. "The fact that we'll be sharing the same cottage isn't the problem here." His grip on the steering wheel was so tight that she marveled that it hadn't collapsed under the intense pressure. "What's troubling you is that we'd be living a lie. Pretense just isn't part of your nature."

"And it *is* yours?"

"Unfortunately, yes," she admitted with typical aplomb.

Her answer didn't appear to please him. "Then you should take to this charade quite well."

"Probably. For a time I toyed with the idea of being an actress."

"Why didn't you?" He tipped his head to one side inquisitively.

"For obvious reasons." Her fingers fanned the auburn curls falling across her smooth brow. "With this red hair and my temperament, I'd be typecast so easily that I'd hate it after a while."

"That's not the real reason."

His insight shocked her. "No," she admitted slowly with a half smile. "Mom didn't like the idea." It had been the only time in her life that her mother had asked anything of her. She'd been a college freshman when she'd caught the acting bug. A drama class and a small part in the spring production had convinced her that she was meant for the silver screen. As usual, her timing was off. Her mother had taken the announcement with a gentle smile, then nodded calmly at Caroline's decision to enroll in additional drama classes. But when it looked like it was more than a passing fancy, Ruth had taken Caroline out to lunch and asked her to abandon the idea of changing her major to drama. She'd given a long list of reasons, all good ones, but none were necessary. Caroline knew this was important to her mother and had forsaken the idea simply because she'd asked.

The road sign indicating that they were entering the city limits of Brookings came into view, and Ted pulled over to the side of the highway and pulled out his phone, calling up the GPS app.

"What are you doing?"

"Getting the directions."

While he punched buttons, Caroline crossed her arms and asked, "Is there anything else that was said in this morning's conversation that I don't know?"

Glancing up from the screen, Ted regarded her with unseeing eyes. "No, why?"

"You keep dropping more and more tidbits of information. Just how long were you on the phone?"

"Five minutes."

She hated being kept in the dark this way. Circumstances being what they were, she would have preferred knowing what they faced instead of bumping into it bit by bit.

After pulling back onto the road again, Ted took a right-hand turn and followed an obscure side street that led downhill as they approached the beach.

Checking the name printed on the mailbox, Ted stopped in front of a white house with a meticulously kept yard. Azaleas lined the walkway, which was illuminated by the porch light.

Eyeing Stranger, Ted murmured, "Maybe you'd better stay here."

"Of course . . . darling," Caroline whispered seductively and batted her eyelashes.

"Don't forget, your name's Thomasson now."

"Naturally." She couldn't resist a languid sigh.

He rubbed his hand over his eyes. "This situation has all the makings of a nightmare."

"Tell me about it," she grumbled under her breath.

She waited with Stranger beside the car, while Ted knocked on the front door of the white house. He was greeted by a short, dark-haired woman with a motherly look. She cast Caroline a sympathetic smile, and when her husband appeared and began talking to Ted, she hurried over to Caroline.

"I'm Anne Bryant. Charles phoned and told us of the unfortunate circumstances of your visit. Now, don't you worry about a thing. You'll be safe here." She smiled curiously at Stranger, no doubt taken aback by his unkempt condition. "And of course your dog is welcome, too."

"Thank you. I'm sure we'll enjoy it here." Caroline liked Anne immediately and wondered if it was because the loving concern in the older woman's eyes reminded her of her mother.

Ted and Mr. Bryant strolled toward the car, still talking. Ted introduced the other man as Oliver. Together the four of them headed down the steep bluff to the cottage, hauling the suitcases, with Stranger traipsing behind on the narrow pathway and the steep stairs that led the last thirty feet.

"We don't have many visitors this time of year," Anne explained. "And none now, so if you see anyone along the beach it might be best to get back inside. No one knows you're here except Oliver and me."

"Unfortunately there's no cell service around here, but if you need a phone, we've still got a land line," the white-haired Oliver explained.

"What a terrible thing to happen to you on your wedding day."

Ted and Caroline's stricken gazes clashed. She had thought pretending to be a loving wife was going to be so easy, but it wasn't. She hated having to lie to these nice people. Seeming to sense her unease, Ted slipped an arm around her waist and pulled her close to his side. She made the effort to smile up at him, but his mouth curved in an expression that was devoid of enjoyment.

The feel of his arm around her brought with it a welter of emotions. His touch felt warm and gentle, and caused her pulse to trip over itself. When his gaze slid to her lips, she was shocked at the desire that shot through her. She yearned for him to turn her in his arms and kiss her there and then. Mentally shaking herself, she pulled her eyes from his.

"The missus and I feel sorry that things are working out so badly for you two lovebirds."

"Yes," Ted murmured. "We're quite upset ourselves."

"Oliver and I wanted to do something special for you to make your wedding night something to remember," Anne continued. "So we spruced up this cottage and turned it into a honeymoon suite."

"Oh, please," Caroline gasped. "That wasn't necessary."

"We thought it was," Oliver said with a delighted chuckle as he swung open the door to the small cottage.

A fire burned in the fireplace, casting a romantic light across the room. A bottle of champagne rested in a bucket of ice on the coffee table, flanked by two wineglasses.

"Now," Oliver said, stepping aside, "you kiss your bride and carry her over the threshold, and we'll get out of your way."

EIGHT

Anne's look was as tender as a dewy rose petal when Ted slid his arm around Caroline's waist and effortlessly lifted her into his arms. His lips nuzzled her ear.

"If you ever wanted to be an actress, the time is now," he whispered.

Looping her arms around his neck, she tossed a grateful glance over her shoulder and laughed gaily. "Thank you both for making everything so special."

"The pleasure was ours," Oliver

said as he pulled his wife close to his side.

"We'll never forget this, will we, darling?" Caroline batted her thick lashes at Ted.

"Never," he grumbled, then stepped inside the cottage as she waved farewell to their hosts. He closed the door with his foot. Almost immediately her legs were abruptly released. Her shoes hit the floor with a loud clump. "Good grief, how much do you weigh?"

She decided to ignore the question. "This is a fine mess you've gotten us into."

"Me?" he snapped. "I told you, I didn't have anything to do with this wedding day business."

"Whatever." As she stomped into the tiny kitchen, she was met with the most delicious aroma. She paused, closed her eyes and took in the fascinating smells before peeking inside the oven. A small rib roast was warming, along with large baked potatoes wrapped in aluminum foil. An inspection of the refrigerator revealed a fresh tossed green salad and two thin slices of cheesecake.

Silence filled the room, and the sound of the refrigerator closing seemed to reverberate against the painted walls.

A scratch on the front door reminded her that Stranger was impatiently waiting outside with their luggage. By the time she returned to the living room, Ted had let the dog inside and was lifting their luggage.

"I'll put your suitcase in the bedroom," he announced.

She was too tired to argue. As her fingers made an unconscious inspection of her blouse buttons, she said, "Dinner is in the oven."

Being ill at ease with each other was easy to understand, given the circumstances. The intimate atmosphere created by the low lights, the flickering fire and the chilling champagne did little to help.

Ted returned from the bedroom and lifted the champagne from its icy bed. A look at the label prompted his brows to arch. "An excellent choice," he murmured, but she had the feeling he wasn't speaking to her. "I'll see about opening this."

The kitchen was infinitely better lighted than the living room, and she opted to remain where she was. With the honeymoon atmosphere slapping them in the face, it would be too easy to pretend this night was something it wasn't. "Okay," she agreed reluctantly.

After turning off the oven, she set the roast out to sit a few minutes before being carved. A quick check of the living room showed Ted working the thin wire wrapping from around the top of the champagne bottle and Stranger sleeping in front of the fireplace. The dog raised his head as the cork shot out of the bottle, but he seemed to realize that he wasn't needed for anything and promptly closed his eyes.

Looking for something to occupy her time and keep her in the kitchen, Caroline turned her attention to the table. She noted that it was already set for two. She busied herself tossing the already-tossed salad and then set it in the center of the table.

Not knowing what else she should do, she stood in the arched doorway and skittishly rubbed the palms of her hands together. "Stranger needs a bath."

"Now?" Ted looked up, holding two filled wineglasses in his hands.

"Yes . . . well, as you may have noticed, he's dirty."

"But the champagne is ready, and from the smell of things, I'd say dinner is, too."

"I believe you also said something about me needing to lose weight. I'll skip dinner tonight," she said stiffly, her voice weakly tinged with sarcasm.

"I didn't say a word to suggest that you're overweight."

"You implied it."

"In that case, I beg your pardon because —" he paused, appraising her intimately "— you're perfect."

Her feet dragging, Caroline stepped into the living room. The fire had died down to glowing red embers, and music was playing softly in the background. She could feel the romantic mood envelop her and had no desire to fight it any longer. What puzzled her most was that Ted had fallen into the mood so easily.

"We've been through a lot together," he commented, handing her a wineglass. "Let's put our differences aside for tonight and enjoy this excellent meal."

She stood nervously to one side. The warm, cozy atmosphere was beginning to work all too well. "It *has* been a crazy day, hasn't it?" She took her first sip and savored the bubbly taste. "This is wonderful."

"I agree," he murmured, sitting on the sofa beside the fireplace.

Reluctantly, Caroline joined him, pausing to pet Stranger.

Ted's gaze fell to the dog, and his startling blue eyes softened. "To be honest, I'm glad he's with us."

"You are?"

"Yes." He stood and added a couple of logs to the fire, then knelt in front of it, poking the embers into flames. Flickering tongues of fire crackled and popped over the bark of the new logs. He stood and turned, but made no effort to rejoin her on the sofa. "Are you enjoying the champagne?"

"Oh, yes." She hugged her arms across her stomach, attempting to ward off her awareness of how close he was to her. She was overly conscious of everything about him. He seemed taller, standing there beside her, and more compelling than she remembered. She could feel the warmth of his body more than the heat of the fire, even though he wasn't touching her.

"I don't think I've ever noticed how beautiful you are," he whispered in a voice so low it was as though he hadn't meant to speak the words aloud.

"Ted, don't," she pleaded, closing her eyes. "I'm not beautiful. Not at all, and I know it." Her hair was much too bright, and those horrible freckles across the bridge of her nose were a humiliation to someone her age. Not to mention her dull brown-green eyes.

"I can't help what I see," he murmured softly, sitting beside her at last. Gently he brushed a stray curl from her face, and then his finger grazed her cheek. Her sensitive nerve endings vibrated with the action, and an overwhelming sensation shot all the way to her stomach with such force that she placed her hand over her abdomen in an effort to calm her reaction. "I've thought so since I first met you."

"Oh?"

"You must have known." His voice remained a husky whisper, creating the impression that this was a moment out of time.

Whatever was happening between them sure beat the constant bickering. They'd done enough of that to last a lifetime. "How could I have known?" she whispered, having difficulty finding her voice. "Sometimes things have to hit me over the head before I notice them."

"I know." He bent his head toward hers, his jaw and chin brushing near her ear.

Caroline's stomach started churning again as his warm breath stirred her silken auburn curls. She gripped the stem of her wineglass so tightly it was in danger of snapping.

Ted pried the glass from her fingers and set it aside. "Relax," his soothing voice instructed. "I'm here to protect you."

She closed her eyes as if to still the quaking sensation, but the darkness only served to heighten her reactions. "Ted," she murmured, not knowing why she'd spoken. His mouth explored the side of her neck, renewing the delicious shivers over her sensitized skin.

"Hmm?"

"Nothing." She slipped her arms around him and rolled her head back to grant him access to any part of her neck he desired. He seemed to want all of it.

A soft moan slipped from her throat when his strong teeth gently nipped her earlobe. The action released a torrent of longing, and she melted against him, repeating his name over and over. If he didn't kiss her soon, she would die.

Somehow he shifted their positions so that she was sitting in his lap. "Here's your champagne," he murmured.

She looked up, surprised. She

wanted his kiss, not the champagne, but when he raised the glass to her lips, she sipped rather than protesting. When she'd finished, his eyes continued to hold hers as he took a drink from the same glass. As he set the champagne aside, his smoky blue eyes paused to take in the look of longing she was convinced must be written on her face for him to see. He cupped her cheek, his fingers sliding down the delicate line of her jaw to rest on the rounded curve of her neck. Then he dipped his head and kissed the corner of her mouth. She yearned to intercept the movement and meet his lips, but she felt like a rag doll, trapped by her strange emotions.

At last his mouth claimed hers in a study of patience. Her breath faltered; she was choked up inside. The kiss was a long, slow process, as he worked his way from one side of her lips to the other, nibbling, tasting, exploring, until Caroline wanted to cry out with longing. When she attempted to deepen the contact and slant her mouth over his, he wouldn't let her. "There's no hurry," he whispered.

"So . . . dinner?" she mumbled, not knowing why. The only appetite she had was for him.

"More of this later," he promised, and leisurely kissed her again.

His mouth, she decided, was far headier than the champagne and twice as potent.

"You're so very beautiful," he whispered.

"Thank you," she mumbled.

He kissed her again, his mouth lingering on her lips as though he couldn't get enough of the taste of her. She didn't mind. She loved it when he kissed her. He was so gentle and caring that the emotions swelled up in her until she wanted to cry with wanting him. When he raised his head, she noted that his eyes were a darker blue when they met the troubled light in hers. He inhaled, attempting to control his desire. With unhurried ease he carefully lifted her off his lap and set her back on the couch.

"Did you say something about dinner being ready?"

Reluctantly, she glanced toward the kitchen. "It can wait a few more minutes."

"Maybe," he agreed. "But I can't. If

we don't stop this soon, I'm going to carry you into that bedroom, and it won't be for sleep."

"Oh," she muttered, and twin blossoms of color invaded her cheeks. She practically leaped off the couch in her eagerness to escape. Hurrying into the kitchen, she went about the dinner preparations without thought. Thinking would have reminded her how much she wanted Ted to touch her, to kiss her. If he hadn't stopped when he did, she would have gone with him into that bedroom. Love did crazy things to people, made them weak — and strong. During all the years of repeatedly saying no to every boyfriend, she had never come so close to surrendering to a man. Heaven knew Clay had tried to get her into bed with him, and although she'd cared for him, she had never been tempted to give him what he wanted most. If he had been more subtle about his desire, she might have succumbed. In the end, when he'd broken off their relationship, he'd used the fact that she hadn't given in to him physically as an excuse, claiming she was a cold fish, not a real woman at all. Challenging her femininity had been the worst possible tack to take if he'd still hoped to get what he wanted. If Ted had lifted her in his arms and carried her into the bedroom, she knew in her heart that she wouldn't have resisted. She'd wanted him and would have willingly given him what so many others had sought.

Ted joined her a few minutes later, standing awkwardly behind her in the close confines of the kitchen. "Is there anything I can do to help?"

For one insane moment she was tempted to ask him to hold her again, kiss her — and make passionate love to her. Thankfully, she suppressed the urge.

The atmosphere at the dinner table was strained. They ate in silence, and although the meal was wonderful, she didn't have much of an appetite.

"Caroline?" Ted said at last, avoiding her eyes as he sank his knife into the roast beef as if he wasn't sure if he should kill it before taking a bite.

"Yes?"

"You mentioned this man you were seeing recently. Did the two of you . . . I mean . . ."

"Are you asking if I'm a virgin?" She would rather swallow fire than admit that to him.

He glared at her, and she nearly laughed. "Are you?"

"That's a pretty personal thing to ask a man."

"But it's all right for a man to ask a woman?"

"In this case, yes."

Caroline sliced her meat so hard it nearly slid off the plate, but a smile hovered just below the surface. "Why do you want to know?"

"Because we nearly . . ."

"Did it," she finished for him. "You needn't worry, I was in complete control the entire time."

"That's not the impression I got."

She ignored that and said, "We make a good team."

"Yes, we do," he agreed, and the amusement in his vivid eyes threw her further off balance then she was already. "And you've already given me the answer to my question."

"I sincerely doubt you know what you're talking about." She swallowed and boldly met his gaze, not giving an inch.

Looking pleased with himself, he pushed his plate aside and leaned back, crossing his arms over his chest. "No woman blushes the way you do if she's accustomed to having a man appreciate her beauty, and you are definitely beautiful."

"You sound awfully sure of yourself."

"Because I am," he said with maddening calm.

Caroline took twice the time necessary to clean the kitchen after dinner.

Giving Stranger a bath and cleaning the bathroom afterward took up even more time. By the time she'd finished three hours later, she was exhausted. Avoiding Ted could become a full-time occupation, she realized. But she couldn't trust her reaction to him, and being alone with him in the small cottage made the situation all the more intolerable.

He was watching television when she reappeared with a thick towel draped over her arm. Stranger traipsed along damply behind her and eyed Ted dolefully. The dog seemed to be asking him what he'd been up to while they were gone. The dog paused in the middle of the room and shook his body with such force that water droplets splattered across the room.

"Hey, what's going on?" Ted asked, brushing at the wet spots on his shirt.

"Sorry," Caroline murmured, hiding a smile.

"Things must be bad when you apologize for a dog," he teased. His eyes grew warm and gentle, and she glanced away rather than risk drowning in their deep blue depths. "You look beat."

"I am." She sat on the floor in front of the fireplace, leaned the back of her neck against the couch and studied the ceiling.

Ted didn't continue with the conversation. She supposed that he was caught up in his television program. She opened one eye, noted what was on and groaned inwardly. He was watching televised fishing — and liking it.

"Ted, since we're asking each other personal questions . . ."

"We are?"

"You know, like the one you asked me at dinner."

"Oh. That."

"Yes, that. Now I have a question for you."

"All right."

He was too agreeable, but she didn't want to turn around and read his expression. "Do you remember the night you dropped me off at the apartment and left because of an appointment?"

"I remember." Reluctance coated his voice.

"Were you telling the truth when you said you weren't seeing a woman?"

It took him so long to answer that

she grew concerned.

Finally he said, "No, to be honest, I lied that night. I didn't have an appointment."

Caroline straightened, giving up all pretense of resting. "You lied?" She would have sworn that he was the most honest man in the world. To have him admit to lying was so out of character that it left her feeling shocked. "But why?"

A muscle close to his eye twitched as he tightly clasped his hands. "We were both feeling a bit unsure that night, and the truth is, I was afraid if I stuck around much longer, drinking coffee and sharing a meal, I wouldn't be going home until morning."

Abruptly Caroline closed her eyes and resumed her earlier position. The way she'd been feeling that night lent credence to his observation. She'd wanted him to stay so badly. "I see."

"At the time I was sure you didn't."

"I thought you preferred not to be with me."

He draped his hand over her shoulder, and she raised hers so that they could lace their fingers together. "Rarely have I wanted anything more than I wanted to be with you that night," he whispered, and bent forward to kiss the crown of her head.

Caroline's heart beat wildly against her rib cage as her brain sang a joyous song. She dared not move, fearing a repeat of what had happened earlier. The realization that Ted found her physically attractive pleased her, but he'd given no indication that his heart was involved.

"I'm going to bed," she announced on the tail end of a long and exquisitely fake yawn. She needed an excuse to leave and think things through.

"Stay," he prompted gently. "The best part of the program is coming up. In a minute they're going to show how to tie flies."

She grimaced. "Isn't that inhumane?"

"Not those kinds of flies," he chided, squeezing her fingers. He urged her up on the sofa so that she ended up sitting beside him. His smiling eyes met hers as he looped an arm around her shoulders.

To her amazement, the fly-tying part of the program was interesting. Bits of feather and fishing line were wrapped around a hook, disguising it so cleverly that she actually had difficulty seeing the hook. But finally, after a series of very real yawns, she couldn't keep her eyes open a minute longer.

"Go to bed," he urged with such tenderness that she had to fight the urge to ask him to come with her. Struggling to her feet, she paused midway across the room. "Where do you want to sleep?"

Without so much as glancing away from the television, he replied, "The better question would be where *will* I sleep?"

"All right," she whispered, embarrassed. She was infuriated with herself for the telltale color that roared into her cheeks. "Where will you sleep?"

"Here."

He was several inches too long for the sofa, but the choice was his, and she was much too fatigued to argue. Tomorrow night she would insist that he take the bed, and she would sleep on the sofa.

A moment later, sitting on the end of the mattress, she yawned again. She really was exhausted. The day had begun early, and it had been long and tiring. It didn't seem possible that so much had happened since they'd left Seattle.

After gathering blankets and a pillow, she contained a deep sigh as she walked back into the living room and wordlessly set them on the far end of the sofa where Ted was still sitting. He was so engrossed in his program that he didn't even seem to notice.

Back in the bedroom a few minutes

later, after quickly washing up, she didn't waste time before putting on her nightgown and climbing between the clean, crisp sheets. Almost immediately after she rested her head on the pillow, the living room lights went out.

"Good night, Ted," she called.

"Night."

A minute later she was wandering in the nether land between sleep and reality. Then the bedroom door creaked open, and her heartbeat went berserk. Had Ted changed his mind and decided to join her? She wanted him. Oh, dear heaven, she wanted him with her. Every night for the remainder of her life she wanted him.

Her courage failed her, and she dared not open her eyes. She would play it cool, she decided, and wait until he was beside her before turning into his arms and telling him all the words that were stored in her heart. But nothing happened. Silence reigned until she couldn't tolerate it a minute longer. As she eased herself up on one elbow, her eyes searched the darkened room. Perplexed, she wondered at the tricks her mind was playing on her. She'd heard the door open. She was sure of it.

A soft whimper came from the floor and, shocked, she tugged the blanket up to her nose as Stranger laid his snout on top of the mattress, seeming to seek an invitation to join her.

"No, boy," she whispered. "You'll have to stay on the floor. This place beside me is reserved for someone else." Then she rested her head back on the thick feather pillow and promptly fell asleep.

Sunlight splashed through the window, and Caroline stirred, feeling warm and content. Long after she was awake, she lay in the soft comfort of the bed and let the events of last evening run through her mind. Ted had held her and kissed her. He'd desired her the other night when he left her, inventing an excuse because he feared he would end up spending the night with her. He'd desired her then, and he wanted her now. Knowing that was better than any dreamy fantasy.

Stranger scratched at the door, wanting out, and she tossed aside the blanket and quickly dressed. A happy smile lit up her face as she pulled jeans up over her hips and snapped

them at her waist. She felt rejuve-
nated after a good night's sleep and
was eager to spend the day with Ted.
For the first time she looked forward
to their time together, almost hoping
that days would stretch into weeks.
This picturesque cottage by the sea
would become their own private
world, where they would learn to
overcome their differences. "Opposites attract" was an old saying,
one she had heard most of her life.
The strong attraction she felt for Ted
was living proof. They were powerfully and overwhelmingly fascinated
with each other. This time together
would teach them the give and take
of maintaining a solid relationship.

As she entered the living room, the
happiness drained from her eyes. The
cottage was empty. The blankets were

neatly folded at the end of the sofa, and for an instant she wondered if they'd even been used. Then she realized that Ted wouldn't have abandoned her; she knew him well enough to realize that. His sense of chivalry wouldn't allow him to leave her alone and unprotected.

Stranger had gone to sit patiently by the front door, wanting out. Feeling hurt and a little piqued at finding Ted gone, she opened the front door. Surprise caused her eyes to widen when she realized that it had been left unlocked. Anyone could have walked in. So this was the protection Ted offered her!

In the kitchen, she discovered that the coffee was made and had been sitting there long enough to have a slightly burned taste. A note propped against the salt shaker on the table informed her that Ted had gone grocery shopping. She knew it was ridiculous to feel so offended, but she was the one who'd gone through two years of training to become a chef. If anyone should do the grocery shopping, it was her. Or they could have had fun doing it together.

Her appetite gone, she went to try her cell and discovered that the Bryants hadn't been kidding. No bars. She pulled a sweater over her head and hiked the trail up to the Bryants' house.

Anne was outside, on her knees, pulling weeds from the flower beds. "Morning," she said cheerfully, awkwardly rising to her feet. She gave Caroline a wry smile. "These old bones of mine are complaining again, but I do so love my flowers."

"They're beautiful." One looked at the meticulously kept yard revealed the love and care each blade of grass and plant was given.

"Can I help you with something? Your husband was by earlier."

For a wild second Caroline had to stop and think of who Anne was talking about. "I'd like to use the phone, if that's all right." In the rush to leave Seattle, she had neglected to make arrangements to have her mail picked up. Mrs. Murphy lived down the hall and would willingly collect it for her. They had each other's mail key for just such instances as this. Normally there wasn't much to worry about, but Caroline had filled out applications for jobs at several restaurants and was hoping employment was in the offing. The sooner she became self-sufficient, the sooner she could prove to her father that she had made the right choice. If she couldn't be reached by phone, then an employer would probably contact her by mail. At least she sincerely hoped so.

"Go right in and help yourself to the phone. It's there on the kitchen wall."

"Thanks."

Stranger followed her to the back door and stayed outside while she made the quick call. Just before she hung up, she asked Mrs. Murphy to mail a smoked salmon from the Pike Place Market to the Bryants as a thank-you for all they'd done. Mrs. Murphy said she would be pleased to do it and didn't mind waiting until Caroline was home to be reimbursed.

On her way back to the cottage, Caroline stopped to chat. Anne explained that Brookings was famous for its azaleas. The flowers were in full bloom in May, and Anne spoke with pride of their beauty. Native azalea bushes covered more than thirty acres of a state park north of town, and Caroline hoped that she would have the opportunity to see them in bloom someday.

The cottage felt empty without Ted. To kill time, she took Stranger for a long walk, trying to teach him to fetch by throwing a stick she found along the way. Anyone observing her would have found her efforts hilarious, she mused sometime later as she sat on a driftwood log, watching the waves come crashing in to shore. No matter how long she stayed, the sight would never bore her. Stranger lay at her feet, panting. Despite that, he was eager for more, as he demonstrated by offering her his stick.

When she heard her name carried by the wind, she turned and waved. Ted jogged to her side, then sank to the sand at her feet. "You weren't at the cabin."

"Brilliant observation," she said with a hint of a smile.

"I thought I told you that I didn't want you running off?"

So they were about to start their day with an argument. She didn't want that. Their time together should be spent building a relationship.

"I didn't run off." The denial was quick, although she strove to appear indifferent.

"I couldn't find you," he returned.

The words were sharp enough to sound like an accusation.

"If you were afraid the boogie man was going to get me, then you might have locked the door."

"Caroline . . ." He turned to her in a burst of impatience and rubbed the back of his neck. "Listen to me. I had to get out of the house this morning."

"Why? We would have had a good time doing the shopping together. I like to cook, remember? I *am* a chef, you know."

"I know." He leaped to his feet and began pacing back and forth in front of her. His steps were quick and sharp, kicking up sand. "Listen, Caroline, we're going to have to help one another. I can't be around you without wanting you. If I'm going to resist, then you'll have to help."

A warm glow of happiness seeped into her blood. "But, Ted," she whispered seductively. "Who says I wanted you to resist?"

NINE

"I wish you hadn't said that," Ted said. He stood looking toward the rolling waves that crashed against the beach. "Being together like this creates enough temptations without you adding to them."

He sounded so stiff and resolute that Caroline wanted to shake him. "So what do you want me to do?" she asked, trying not to sound too defensive. "Sleep in the car or camp out on the beach?"

"Don't be silly."

"Me be silly? I thought you knew

me better than that." She picked up a handful of the sand and slowly let it slip through her fingers. The grains felt gritty and damp. She'd awakened with such high expectations for this day, and already things were beginning to fall apart.

Lowering himself onto the log beside her, he claimed her hand with his. "The problem isn't you," he admitted with a wry twist of his mouth. "I'm the one having difficulties. It's nothing you've done — or not intentionally, anyway. You can't help it if I find your smile irresistible." He bent his head toward her and tucked a strand of hair behind her ear. "And you have the most incredible eyes."

She could feel the color working its way up to her face but was powerless to resist when he lowered his head and tenderly explored the side of her neck, sending delicious shivers skittering down her spine. Her stomach was tightening as waves of longing lapped through her. Her fingers clawed against the wood as she resisted the urge to slide her arms around him and lose herself in his embrace.

"See what I mean?" he groaned. "I can't even be close to you without wanting to kiss you."

"But I want you to touch me," she whispered candidly.

"I know."

"Is that so bad?" she asked in a prompting voice, leaning her head on his shoulder. "You make me feel beautiful."

"You *are* beautiful."

"Only to you."

"Is the world so blind?"

"No," she returned softly. "You are."

His hand found her hair. Braiding his fingers through the thick length of it, he pressed her closer to him. "That's my greatest fear."

"What is?"

"That what's happening between us isn't real. I'm afraid that circumstances have put us under unnatural stress. It's only logical that our feelings would become involved."

"Are you saying that I'm not feeling what I think I'm feeling?" She cocked her head a bit and grinned. "That doesn't make sense, does it?"

"The problem is that, as a couple, *we* don't make sense."

"Oh." She swallowed down the

hurt. "I thought we balanced one another out rather well."

"Maybe, but that's something we won't know until this ordeal is over. As it is, we're playing with dynamite."

"What do you suggest, then?" She was sure she wasn't going to like anything he proposed.

"No touching. No kissing. No flirting."

"Oh." She straightened, lifting her head from his shoulder as a chill that had nothing to do with the weather ran through her. "Nothing?"

"Nothing," he confirmed.

She ran her fingers through her hair, not caring about the tangles. She needed something to do with her hands.

"Do you agree?"

There was little else she could do.

"All right, but I don't like it."

"Constantly being together isn't going to make this easy." He clenched his jaw and shook his head. "But that can't be helped."

Ted had made her feel lovely and desirable. When he'd held her, it hadn't mattered that her eyes were dull and her nose had freckles. To him, in those brief moments, she had been Miss Universe. Now she felt as if she had a bad case of the measles.

"I — I think I'll put away the groceries," she said, rising to her feet and pausing to wipe the sand from the back of her jeans. "Is there anything special you'd like for lunch?" She couldn't look at him for fear he would read the misery in her eyes.

"No," he answered on a solemn

note. "Anything is fine."

Caroline spent the remainder of the morning in the kitchen, baking a fresh lemon meringue pie and a loaf of braided holiday bread. Heavenly smells drifted through the cottage. She loved to bake. From the time she was a child, she'd enjoyed mixing up a batch of cookies or surprising her mother with a special cake. Kneading bread dough was therapeutic for her restless mind. She thought about her relationship with Clay and was surprised to realize that the pain of their breakup was completely gone now. She was grateful for the good times they'd shared, but he'd been right — she simply hadn't loved him enough. He'd asked her to prove her love — admittedly, in all the wrong ways — and she'd balked. Her hesitation had caused the split, and for a time it had hurt so much that she had wondered if she'd done the right thing. But she had. She knew that because now she was in love, really in love, with no doubts or insecurities. But Ted doubted. Ted was filled with uncertainties. Ted wanted them to wait and be sure. How like him to be cautious, and how typical of her to be impulsive and impatient.

By evening a plan had formed. Bit by bit, day by day she would prove to him that they weren't really so different. They shared plenty of things in common, and she simply needed to accentuate those. Within a few days he would realize that she would make him the perfect wife. She would cook fantastic meals, be enthralled by what he had to say, and laugh at his corny jokes. Within a week he would be on bended knee with stars in his eyes. In fact, she was shocked that he didn't see how perfect they were together. They'd been meant for each other from the time they were teenagers. Unfortunately, circumstances had led them apart, but no longer.

Dusk had settled when Ted returned to the cottage, hauling in an armload of wood for the fireplace. She had wondered what he'd done with himself all afternoon. He'd eaten lunch with her, then left almost immediately afterward. She hadn't seen him since, but Stranger had gone with him and returned at his side now.

"Something smells good," Ted commented, setting the uniformly cut logs on the hearth.

Wiping her hands on the terry-cloth apron she'd found in a drawer, she joined him in the living room. "I hope you like pot roast in burgundy wine with mushrooms."

His brows arched appreciatively. "I don't know, but it sounds good."

"I would have attempted something more elaborate, but . . ."

"No, no, that sounds fantastic."

"There's homemade bread, and fresh lemon meringue pie for dessert." After days of traveling and living together, she suddenly felt awkward and a little shy. She hadn't been bashful a day in her life, so this reaction was completely out of character for her.

He didn't look any more confident about their arrangement than she felt. They stood with only a few feet separating them, both looking miserable and unsure. "I'll wash my hands if everything's ready," he murmured after an awkward moment.

"It is."

At the dinner table they sat across from each other, but neither one of them spoke. Caroline literally didn't know what to say. The silence was thick enough to taste. Again and again her gaze was drawn to him, and every cell in her body was aware of him sitting so close, and yet they were separated by something more powerful than distance. Once she glanced up to discover him studying her, and her breath caught. He looked away sharply, as though he were angry at being caught. But if he was looking at her with half the interest with which she was viewing him, then they were indeed in for trouble.

The next morning Caroline woke to find that once again Ted had already left the cottage. The pattern repeated itself in the days that followed. She could sometimes see him working in the distance, chopping wood. What else he did to occupy his time, she didn't know, and she had no idea what the Bryants thought of a honeymoon couple who barely spent time together. Evenings proved to be both their worst and their best times. Since she did all the cooking, he insisted on cleaning the kitchen. At times she was convinced he only volunteered because it limited the time they spent in close proximity to each other.

To their credit, they both did their

best to put aside their almost magnetic attraction. And despite everything, there were times when she could almost believe things were natural and right between them. Ted taught her how to play backgammon and chided her about beginner's luck when she proceeded to win every game. Later they switched to chess. Oddly enough, they discovered that although their strategies were dissimilar, their skills were evenly matched. When their interest turned to cards, she insisted that he play poker with her. He agreed, as long as she was willing to learn the finer techniques of bridge. One evening of poker and bridge was enough for her to realize that cards was one area they would do better to ignore.

Some nights they read. Ted's tastes

were so opposite to her own that she found it astonishing that she could love such a man. And love him she did, until she wanted to burst. Doing as he'd asked and avoiding any physical contact had proven to her how much she did care for him. He seemed so staid and in control. Only an occasional glance told her that his desire for her hadn't lessened. When he looked at her, all the warmth he had stored in his heart was there for her to see. Some nights she wanted to cry with frustration, but she'd agreed to this craziness, and in time her plan would work. It was taking far longer than she'd expected, though.

Late nights, when the cottage was dark and she lay in bed alone, proved to be the most trying times. They were separated by only a thin door that was often left ajar so Stranger could wander in and out at will. Some nights, when she lay perfectly still, she could hear the rhythmic sound of Ted's even breathing. She wanted to be with him so much that sleep seemed impossible and she lay awake for hours.

Seven days after they'd arrived in Brookings, Caroline had experienced enough frustration to last her ten lifetimes. True to his word, Ted hadn't touched her. Not even so much as an accidental brushing of their hands. He seemed to take pains to avoid being near her. If she was in the kitchen, he stayed in the living room. After dinner, he lingered in the other room so long she had to call him into the living room for their nightly games. It was almost as if he dreaded spending any time with her and each minute together tried his resolve. Yet in her heart she knew that he desired her, wanted to be with her, and hated this self-imposed discipline with as much intensity as she did.

On the afternoon of the eighth day, she was finished baking a cake and had set it out to cool before frosting it. Surely by now he could see what fantastic wife material she was, she thought. If he didn't, then she would be forced to take matters into her own hands. But she would much prefer it if he recognized his love for her without forcing her to resort to more . . . forceful methods.

The sun was bathing the earth in golden light when Caroline pulled on a thin sweater. In moments she was on the beach, where Stranger came racing to her side, kicking up sand in his eagerness to join her.

"Hiya, boy." She sank to her knees and ruffled his ears as he demonstrated his affection. From the way he was behaving, an observer would have assumed they'd been separated for weeks.

More by accident than design, Stranger had become Ted's dog. In the beginning she hadn't even been sure he wanted the dog tagging along after him. He neither encouraged nor discouraged the dog. Stranger simply went.

What Ted did during the days was a thorn in Caroline's side. Not once had he mentioned where he went, although she had phrased the question in ten different ways and with as much diplomacy as possible. He would smile and look right through her, then direct the conversation in another direction. Her curiosity was piqued. There was nothing to do but wait impatiently for him to explain himself in his own time, which he would — or she would torture it out of him.

Petting Stranger, she noticed that he was wearing a collar. She did know that Ted had taken the dog to a veterinarian in town one afternoon and she'd been pleased to learn he was suffering no ill effects from his days as a stray. Later she'd discovered a doggie toy that Ted had obviously bought.

"Stranger," she whispered, elated, "I love him. I really do. I think it's as much of a surprise to me as anyone," she said, and ran her hand through the dog's thick fur. "You love him, too, don't you, boy?"

The dog cocked his head at her inquisitively and she thought how strange it was that she could talk so freely to him.

"Come on, let's go for a walk." Agilely, she rose to her feet. Maybe she would stumble on Ted and discover his deep, dark secret. Surely he spent his days doing more than chopping wood. By now he'd chopped enough to supply the cottage for two long winters. After an hour's jaunt up and down the sandy shore, Caroline was convinced he wasn't anywhere around.

As she started back to the cottage, Anne waved to her from the top of the bluff. The two often shared a cup of coffee in the afternoon, and Caroline waved in return and started up the creaky walkway.

"The salmon arrived this afternoon. I can't thank you enough."

"Ted and I wanted you to know how much we appreciate everything you've done."

"You're such a sweet couple. It's obvious that you two were meant to be together."

Obvious to everyone but Ted. "What a nice thing to say," Caroline murmured, glancing at the green grass between her feet.

"At first I was concerned, I don't mind telling you. It didn't seem right that a honeymoon couple spent so much time apart. Your husband painting, and you down there in that cottage cooking your heart out."

So Ted was painting. Probably helping Oliver out every day just so he could avoid being with her.

"He's so talented. When I saw the beach scene he did of you and the dog, I was utterly amazed. Oliver offered to buy it, he liked it so much. But Ted refused — said it wasn't for sale."

Caroline's head shot up. Ted was an artist! He'd never said a word to her, not a word. So that was what he did with his time. And he'd shown Anne his work, but not her. An unbearable weight pressed against her heart, and she swallowed back the bitter taste of discouragement. "He's wonderful," she agreed weakly.

"Do you have time for coffee?"

"Not today, Anne. Sorry."

"Thanks again for the salmon."

With her hands buried deep inside her pockets, Caroline started walking along the top of the bluff. If Ted was painting, he was probably doing it from this vantage point.

"Caroline!" Anne called, pointing in the opposite direction. "Ted's over that way."

"Of course, thanks," she returned, and gave a brief salute.

Stranger raced on ahead. She rounded a curve in the windswept landscape and hesitated when she saw Ted. He was so caught up in what he was doing that he didn't notice her until she was only a few feet away. When he did see her, he glanced up and a look of incredible guilt masked his features.

"Is anything wrong?" he asked.

"No." She laced her fingers in front of her and looked out over the beach below. The cottage was in clear sight, and there was a long stretch of beach on either side, so that no matter where she walked, he could see her. "It's lovely from up here, isn't it?"

"Yes," he said and swallowed. "It is."

"I hope I'm not interrupting you," she lied.

"No, not at all." He set his easel aside and stood so that he was blocking her view of the canvas.

Caroline got the message louder than if he'd shouted it. He didn't want her looking at his painting any more than he wanted her to be there. "I just came up to say hello, and — and now that I've done that I'll be on my way."

"You can stay if you want."

She didn't believe a word of his insincere invitation. "No thanks. I've . . . I've got things to do at the cottage." Like count dust particles and watch the faucet drip.

"I'll be down in time for dinner."

Her answer was a hurried nod as she turned sharply and retreated with quick-paced steps that led her away from him with such haste that she nearly slipped on the path leading down the bluff to the cottage.

Stranger elected to stay with Ted, seeming to sense her troubled mood and her desire to be alone. The pain of Ted's simple deception hurt so much she could hardly bear it.

All this time that they'd been together, she'd been open and honest with him. She trusted him implicitly.

While waiting for him to make his moves in chess, she'd shared her dreams and all the things that were important to her. One night in particular, when neither of them had been sleepy, they'd sat in front of the fireplace, drinking spiced apple cider. They'd ended up talking away half the night. She had never felt closer to anyone. That night had convinced her that what she felt for Ted was a woman's love, a love that was meant to last a lifetime. Unwittingly she'd given him her heart that night, handed it to him on a silver platter. Not until now did she realize that she'd been the one doing all the talking. He had shared a little about his life; he'd spoken of his job and a few other unimportant items but revealed little about himself. He certainly hadn't mentioned the fact that he painted or even that he appreciated art. She'd admired the canvases on his apartment walls and realized with a flash of renewed pain that he'd probably done those, as well. Anne was right. Ted was a talented artist.

He found her about four-thirty, sitting on the beach, looking out over the pounding surf. He lowered himself beside her, but she didn't acknowledge his presence.

"You're looking thoughtful."

"I'm bored," she murmured. "I want to go home."

He forcefully expelled his breath. "Caroline, I'm sorry, but we can't."

He'd probably been talking to Randolph again and not telling her about it. Ted liked keeping secrets.

"Not we — me! I'm the one who's

going."

"What brought this on?"

Staring straight ahead, yet blind to the beauty that lay before her, Caroline shook her head. "Eight days stuck in a cottage with no contact with the outside world is enough for anyone to endure."

"I thought you liked it here," he countered sharply. "I had the impression you were having a good time."

She leaned back, pressing her weight onto the palms of her hands, and raised her face to the sky. "I told you before I was a good actress."

"So this whole time together was all an act." A thread of steel ran through his words.

"What else?" She could feel the hard flint of his eyes drilling into her.

"I don't believe that, Caroline, not

for a minute."

She gave an indifferent shrug. "Think what you want, but I'm leaving."

"No you aren't."

Clenching her jaw so hard that her teeth hurt, she refused to argue. She would leave. Finding someplace else, any place away from Ted, was essential. He had discovered a place within her where only he could cause her pain. If he'd wanted to punish her for the sins of her youth, he'd succeeded. She'd never felt so cold and alone, so emotionally drained or unloved. She had given him a part of herself that she had never before shared, only to learn that he didn't trust her enough to trust her with that same part of himself.

When she chanced a look at Ted,

his expression of mixed anger and bewilderment tugged at her heart. The best thing for them both would be for her to leave as quickly as possible before they continued to hurt each other.

"I'll go wash up for dinner," he announced, rolling to his feet with subtle ease.

She refused to look up at him. "I didn't cook anything."

"I'll do it, then."

"Do whatever you want, but only cook for one."

He ignored the gibe. "Come on."

"Where?"

"You're coming to the house with me."

"I thought you said you were going to fix your own dinner?"

"I am, but I don't want you out

here alone."

"Why not? You leave me alone every day."

His hand under her arm roughly pulled her up from the sand. "I'm not going to argue with you. You're coming with me."

Jerking her arm aside to free herself from his touch, she took a step backward. Stranger gave the two of them an odd look, tilting his head, unaccustomed to their raised voices.

"You're confusing the dog," she said.

"The dog?" Ted shot back. "You're confusing *me*."

"Good." Maybe he would feel some of the turmoil that was troubling her. Trying to give an impression of apathy, she rubbed the sandy grit from her hands, feeling more wretched every second.

"Good?" Ted exploded. "Why do you want to do this to me? Just what kind of game are you playing?"

"I'm not playing a game. I just want out." To her horror, her voice cracked and tears welled up, brightening her eyes. She shoved her hands in her pockets and started toward the cottage.

"Caroline."

She quickened her pace.

"Caroline, stop! You're going to listen to me for once."

"I'm through listening!" she shouted, wiping away a tear and fighting to hold back the others. When she heard his footsteps behind her, she started to run. She didn't have any destination in mind, she only knew she had to escape.

His hand on her shoulder whirled her around, throwing her off balance. A cry of alarm slid from her throat as she went tumbling toward the sand. Ted wrapped his arms around her and twisted so that he accepted the brunt of the fall. Quickly he changed positions so that she was half-pinned beneath him.

"Are you all right?"

A scalding tear rolled from the corner of her eye, and she averted her face. "Yes." Her voice was the weakest of whispers.

Gently, with infinite patience, he wiped the maverick tear from her cheek. His hands were trembling slightly as he cupped her face. "Caroline," he whispered with such tenderness that fresh tears misted her eyes. "Why are you crying?"

348

Unable to answer him, she slowly shook her head, wanting to escape and in the same heartbeat wanting him to hold her forever.

"I don't think I've ever seen you upset like this." He smoothed the hair from her face. "You've got to be the bravest, gutsiest woman I've ever known. It's not like you to cry."

"What do you care if I cry?" she sniffled, shocked at how unnatural her voice sounded.

"Trust me, I care."

Not believing him, she closed her eyes and turned her face away from his penetrating gaze. Her hands found his shoulders and she tried to push him away, but he wouldn't let her.

"Caroline," he groaned in frustration. "I care. I've always cared about you. I want you so much it's tying me up in knots so tight I think . . ." He didn't finish as his mouth crushed down on hers, kissing her with a searing hunger that left her breathless and light-headed.

"Ted," she groaned. "Don't, please don't." Having him touch and kiss her made leaving all the more impossible, and she had to go. For her sanity, she had to get away from him before he claimed any more of her. She'd already given him her heart.

"I've wanted to do that every minute of every day." Again his mouth claimed hers, tasting, moving, licking, until she feared she would go mad with wanting him.

"Ted, no . . . you said . . ." But her protest grew weaker with every word.

He cut off her protest by pressing

his lips against hers, tasting them as though they were flavored with the sweetest honey. The urgency was gone, replaced with a gentleness that melted her bones. She felt soft and loved, and he was male and hard. Opposites. Mismatched. Different.

And yet perfect for each other.

But not perfect enough for him to share a part of himself, she remembered. No, he didn't need her — not nearly enough. With a strength she didn't know she possessed, she pushed against his shoulder, breaking the contact.

Stunned, he sat up, while she remained on the sandy beach, lying perfectly still. Every part of her throbbed with longing until holding back the tears was impossible. She covered her face with her hands.

"I thought you said you wanted me?"

"No," she whispered, sitting up beside him. She looped her arms around her knees and took deep, even breaths to calm her heart.

The muscles in his jaw knotted. "That wasn't the impression you gave me the other night when you invited me to your bed."

"That was the other night." Another lifetime, when she'd felt they'd had a chance.

"And this is now?" he asked with heavy sarcasm.

"Right."

"You don't know what you want, do you? Everything is a game. It doesn't matter who's caught up in your —"

Caroline had heard enough. She

put out a hand to stop him from talking, and then, with a burst of energy she struggled to her feet and rushed inside the cottage. Stranger was lying beside the fireplace, waiting for her.

"You stay here with Ted," she told the dog as she hurried into the lone bedroom and dragged out her empty suitcase.

"I told you I wouldn't let you go," Ted said, his large frame blocking the doorway between the bedroom and the living room.

"You don't have any choice. Please, Ted," she pleaded. "I don't want to argue with you over this. I'm leaving."

"But why now?" he asked firmly. "What makes today any different from yesterday?"

She could hardly tell him the truth,

that her heart was breaking a little bit more every day as it became clear that he would never feel about her as she felt about him. "Because I'm bored, and if I spend one more minute cooped up in this place I'll go crazy," she lied.

Ted ran his fingers through his hair in agitation and then curled his hand around the back of his neck. "I'm sorry. I guess I haven't been very good company."

"That's not it. For Tedious Ted, I'd say you did a fine job, but I want out. Now." Delaying the inevitable would only prolong the pain. She opened the suitcase and began dumping her clothes inside.

"I'm sorry, Caroline, but I can't let you go."

"You don't have any choice." She

would have thought he knew her better than to lay such a challenge at her feet.

"If I need to, I'll tie you up."

"You'll have to."

"I won't have any qualms about doing it."

Her eyes sparked with determination. "You'll have to catch me first."

Ted's gaze hardened. "I can't believe you're doing this."

"Believe it," she said, then slammed the suitcase shut and swung it off the bed.

A loud knock at the front door diverted their attention.

"Stay here," Ted commanded. He checked the window before swinging open the door. "Hello, Oliver, what can I do for you?"

"There's a call for you. Detective

Randolph."

Tossing a look over his shoulder at Caroline, Ted nodded. "I'll be right there." He closed the door and turned to face her.

"Go answer your important call."

"I want your promise you won't try to sneak out of here while I'm on the phone."

Her mouth thinned to a brittle line. "My promise?" He had no right to bring up promises. He'd said he wouldn't touch her, and then he'd kissed her until she'd thought she would die from wanting him. Childishly she crossed her fingers behind her back in an effort to negate her words.

"Caroline, promise me you won't try to leave. Either do that or I'm dragging you up that path with me."

"All right, I won't leave." Her heart ached with the lie.

His facial muscles relaxed. "Thank you. I'll be down to let you know what's happening as fast as I can."

It didn't matter, because the minute he was safely out of sight she was leaving. She didn't like breaking her word, but he had forced her into it.

Emotion clouded her eyes. Checking her purse for cash and credit cards, she decided the best thing to do was to take her chances walking along the beach. For the first few hours she would need to avoid the highway. Eventually she could find a town and rent a car.

She paused only long enough to say goodbye to Stranger and assure the dog that Ted would be good to him.

Her heart tightened as she took one

last look around the cottage. She would always remember these days with Ted as a special time in her life.

She wasn't more than a few feet out of the door when a shadowy figure moved from behind a large rock.

Her heart rose to her throat, and fear coated the inside of her mouth, as the brawny, angry man she'd seen in the courtroom with Joan MacIntosh stepped directly in front of her.

TEN

Caroline felt her panic rise. She was alone and defenseless. She'd intentionally left Stranger inside, afraid that the dog would follow her down the beach. Ted and Oliver wouldn't hear her cries, and, from the size of this man, she doubted that she could outrun him. Her hands felt weak, and she dropped her suitcase to the sand.

He seemed to sense her fear and took a step toward her.

Raising her hands defensively, she met his glare head-on. "I would advise you to leave now. I've taken karate lessons," she said with as much bravado as her thumping heart would allow. She didn't mention that she'd quit after three classes. Her breathing was shallow as she edged backward with small steps, praying he wouldn't notice that she was working her way toward the bluff. If he raced after her, she would have more of an opportunity to escape. At least if she got above him, she would be able to kick at him. In addition, there was a chance Ted would hear what was happening. Somehow, some way, she had to warn him. Otherwise he would come down the bluff to tell her what was going on and walk into a trap.

The man shifted slightly, and his dark shape was outlined by the sun, making it impossible for her to see his face clearly. He looked around, but she couldn't tell what he was thinking. Why had she left Stranger in the cottage? She wanted to reason with her attacker, plead for him to understand, but alarm clogged her throat, and the words tangled helplessly on the end of her tongue.

"Where's Ted Thomasson?"

The heel of her tennis shoe hit the edge of the bottom step, and with a frenzy born of fear and determination she turned, grabbed a handful of sand and threw it in his face. Taking the creaky wooden stairs two at a time, she ran from him, screaming for Ted at the top of her voice.

"Ted! Ted!"

She heard Stranger begin barking wildly and scratching at the front door to get out.

"Caroline!" Miraculously, Ted appeared at the top of the bluff.

"He's here!" she cried. "He found us!" She was trapped between the two men, positioned halfway up the stairs. She turned toward Joan MacIntosh's companion. From this height, she could better see the bulky man. He looked surprised, almost stunned.

Ted raced down the bluff to Caroline's side. "If you've touched a hair on her head," he called to the other man, who hadn't moved, "you'll pay." He put his arm around her, his fingers biting into her side. "Are you all right?" he whispered near her ear.

"Fine, I think," she whispered back.

He attempted to step in front of her, but she wouldn't let him.

"Caroline," Ted groaned with frustration as they juggled for position. "Let me by."

"No," she argued, stepping one way and then another on the narrow stair, blocking him.

"If you two would stop being so willing to die for each other, maybe you could listen to what I've come to say."

"You listen!" Ted shouted, placing his hands on Caroline's shoulders and holding her still. "I just finished talking to Detective Charles Randolph from the Seattle police department. They've caught the man who's responsible for the attacks."

"Was it Nelson Bergstrom?" She twisted around, needing to know.

Ted didn't seem to hear her; his gaze was focused on the man below.

She returned her attention to him as well.

"I know!" he shouted up at them. "I've come to try to make amends to you for everything I've done."

"You mean you don't want to kill us?" she asked, her tensed muscles relaxing in relief.

"Don't act so disappointed," Ted said in a low murmur as he smoothly altered their positions so that he stood directly in front of her.

"So you're the one who kept calling us?" Ted asked.

"Yes." The stranger laced his fingers together in front of him and looked almost boyish as his eyes shone with regret. "And I was the one who spray-painted the outside of your apartment and made those threats." He swallowed and lowered his chin. "I want you to know that I'll pay for any damage."

"We can discuss that later," Ted replied. "For now, it would be best if you returned to Seattle. I'll contact you once we return."

"I *am* sorry."

Caroline felt compassion swelling in her. "I can understand how you felt," she told him, and was rewarded with a feeble smile.

"It's the most helpless feeling in the world to have something like that happen to the person you love most in the world. However, that doesn't make up for the things I did to the two of you. Venting my anger and frustration on you was wrong."

"I understand, and I accept your apology," she said.

"Thank you for that. But I'm ready

to pay for what I did, even if that means going to jail. I deserve it for having put you two through so much. If it's any consolation now, I want you to know I didn't mean any of those threats. That's all they were — empty threats."

"It took courage to come here and face us."

"I had to do something," the man continued. "You can imagine how I felt when the police contacted Joan. The attacker made a full confession. If it had been up to me, I would have condemned an innocent man."

"We did the right thing to let Nelson Bergstrom off," Ted informed her — needlessly, since she'd already figured that out.

"Oh, thank God." Relief washed through her until it overflowed. The guilt she'd experienced when another woman was attacked had been overwhelming. She'd tried to convince herself that following her conscience was the important thing. But that knowledge hadn't relieved the weight of the albatross that had hung around her neck — until now.

"I'll be leaving now. When you want to contact me back in Seattle, the name's John MacIntosh." He turned away and started walking down the beach.

"John!" Ted called, stopping him. "How did you know where to find us?"

Caroline had been wondering the same thing herself.

"Miss Lomax's neighbor told me the address."

"I see," Ted said slowly.

His look narrowed, cutting into Caroline as she searched for the words to exonerate herself. "I gave it to her so she could mail the salmon to —"

"What salmon?"

"— Anne and Oliver as a thank-you for all they'd done."

"You told someone where we were?"

"Just Mrs. Murphy, but I assumed that —"

"I can't believe you'd do something so incredibly stupid. So . . . insane."

"Stupid?" she sputtered almost incoherently, her temper rising. "The dumbest, most insane thing I've ever done is take this crazy trip with you."

"I couldn't agree with you more." Ted stalked down the stairs, leaving her standing there, feeling both humiliated and ashamed. All right, she would concede that giving Mrs. Murphy their address wasn't the smartest thing she'd done in her life, but it was far saner than falling in love with Ted.

He stopped outside the cottage doorway when he found her suitcase in the sand. He hesitated, as if stunned, and a renewed sense of guilt filled her.

He turned and gave her a look of such utter contempt that she knew she would remember it the rest of her life. "So you were planning to leave anyway." He stopped to study her flushed, guilt-ridden face. "Even after you'd given me your word."

"Yes," she admitted, and her chin rose a notch. "Not that it matters anymore. Now that everything's been settled, there's no reason for me to stay." Her lips trembled as she struggled to regain her composure. Without knowing why, she followed Ted inside the cottage and watched as he took out his own suitcase and began to pack. His movements were short and jerky, as if he couldn't finish the task fast enough. He was normally so organized and neat, but now he merely stuffed the clothes inside, then slammed the lid closed.

"I'll tell the Bryants we're leaving."

"Not together we're not," she corrected him briskly. "I'm not going back to Seattle."

"Just where do you plan to go?"

"San Francisco." The name came from the top of her head. Her parents' house would be empty and cold, but she couldn't remain with Ted. She had too much pride for that, and too little self-control. He had to know she loved him. She'd done everything she could to prove she wanted to be his — everything except propose marriage. From the things she'd realized lately, she recognized that he simply didn't want her. The knowledge seared a hole into her heart. She would recover, she told herself repeatedly as she picked up her suitcase and followed him up the creaky old stairs. But her heart refused to listen.

Caroline had assumed that familiar surroundings would lessen the void in her soul. She was wrong. A three-day stint alone in San Francisco had taught her that she couldn't return home like a little girl anymore. She was a woman now, with a woman's hurts. She'd wandered aimlessly around the empty house, and all she could think about was Ted.

He had dropped her off at the airstrip in Brookings and left almost immediately afterward, with Stranger looking forlornly at her from the backseat of the car. She hadn't heard from him since, not that she'd really expected to.

Her return to Seattle a couple of weeks ago had been uneventful. She found part-time employment the first week. Having a job lent purpose to her days and proved to be her salvation.

Her mother telephoned, full of enthusiasm after they returned from China, but for the first time in her adult life, Caroline couldn't bare her soul to her mother.

"For a minute when I walked in the door, I thought you might have come for a visit."

"I *was* in San Francisco, Mom."

"When? Why?"

"It's a long story."

Her mother seemed to sense that Caroline wasn't eager to share the events of her latest escapade. "You don't sound like yourself, honey. Is something wrong?"

"What could possibly be wrong? I've got the very thing I've always wanted. I'm working as a chef and loving it."

"But you don't sound happy."

"I'm . . . just tired, that's all."

"Have you seen any more of Ted Thomasson?"

The pain was so intense that Caroline hesitated before speaking. "No, not for a couple of weeks now." Two weeks, four days and twenty-one hours, she mentally calculated, glancing at her watch.

An awkward silence followed. "Well, I just wanted you to know that your father and I arrived back home safely, and that China was wonderful."

"I'm pleased you're home, Mom. Thanks for calling. I'll give you a ring later in the week."

"Caroline, don't you want to tell your father about your job?"

"You can go ahead and tell him, if you want to."

It wasn't until she hung up that she realized her mistake. At any other time in her life, she would have been puffed up like a bull frog at having achieved her goal of working in a restaurant kitchen. Now her profession was nothing more than a means to fill the empty days.

She'd barely finished the conversation with her mother when a hard knock sounded against her front door. She glanced at it, inexplicably knowing in her heart that Ted stood on the other side. The entire time she'd been back, she had subconsciously been waiting to hear from him. Now, like a coward, she waited until the hard knock was repeated. Forcing a brittle smile to her lips, she finally turned the lock and opened the door.

"Hello, Caroline." His eyes caressed her like a warm, golden flame.

"Hello, Ted. How are you?" Pride demanded that she not reveal any of the emotional pain these weeks apart had cost her. He looked wonderful.

Everything she'd remembered about him seemed even more pronounced now. His features were even more rugged and compelling. His eyes were an even deeper shade of blue, if that were possible. The strong, well-shaped mouth that had shown her such pleasure slanted into a half smile.

"I brought your kite and your other things."

The instant she'd seen what he was carrying, she had realized with a sinking heart that the reason for his visit wasn't personal. "How's Stranger?"

"Fine. My apartment doesn't allow pets, so I had to find a home for him."

"You gave Stranger away?" She breathed in sharply, unbelievably hurt that he would so callously give up their dog.

"Could you take him?"

Her apartment building had the same restriction. "No," she admitted, subdued. "You . . . did the right thing. Is he happy in his new home?"

"Very."

Her smile wavered, and she murmured with a breathless catch in her voice, "Then that's what counts." Realizing that she had left him standing in the doorway, she hurriedly stepped aside. "Come in, please."

"Where do you want me to put all this?"

"The kitchen counter will be fine. Thanks." She threaded her fingers together so tightly that they ached. She knew her features were strained with the burden of maintaining an expression of poise. She tried unsuccessfully to relax.

"Do you still make that fancy coffee?" he asked softly.

"Yes . . . would you like a cup?"

"If you have the time."

Time was something she had plenty of these days. Time to remember how his mouth tasted on hers. Time to recall the velvet smoothness of his touch and how well their bodies fit together. Time to compile a list of regrets that was longer than a rich kid's Christmas list.

Their gazes held for several seconds. "Yes, I have the time," she murmured at last, breaking eye contact.

He followed her into the kitchen. "How have you been?"

"Wonderful," she lied with practiced ease. "I have a job. It's only afternoons for now, but I'm hoping that it'll work into full time later this summer." Actually, she'd taken the first job that was offered, even though she would have preferred a regular forty-hour work schedule. But anything was better than moping around the house day after day.

"I'm pleased things are working out for you."

"What about you?" She couldn't look at him, knowing it would be too painful.

"I've been fine," he supplied, leaning against the kitchen counter.

She put as much space between them as possible in the cozy kitchen. Her gaze centered on the glass pot, praying the water would boil quickly.

"We need to talk," he said quietly.

"You know that, don't you, Caroline?"

She gripped the counter so hard it threatened to break her neatly trimmed nails. "About what?" Wildly she looked away as her heart jammed in her throat.

"About us."

"Us?" She forced a laugh that sounded amazingly like a restrained sob. "Within two hours we were at each other's throats. How can you even suggest there's an 'us'?"

"That's not the way I remember it." The minute the coffee finished brewing, she filled two cups and handed him one. He immediately set it on the counter. "Coffee was only an excuse, and you know it."

She took a quick step away from him. "I wish you'd said something before I went through the trouble of making it."

"No you don't."

Without her noticing, he had moved closer to her, trapping her in a corner. Mere inches separated them. Her breathing had become so shallow it was nearly nonexistent.

"I thought I'd give myself time to sort out my feelings." He lifted the luxurious silky auburn curls away from the side of her neck. Her pulse hammered wildly as his thumb stroked her skin. "Every time I was close to you, I had to fight to keep myself from kissing you."

Magnetically, Caroline's gaze was drawn to his eyes. "It's only natural that under the circumstances we — we feel these — these strong physical attractions."

"Problem is," Ted said softly, his breath caressing her face, "I'm experiencing the same things now, only even more powerfully, more intensely, than ever."

"That can't be true," she insisted, too afraid to believe him and seeking an escape. Abruptly she turned and reached for her coffee, nearly scalding her lips as she took a sip. She clenched the mug with both hands. "What we had on the beach wasn't real," she said in a falsely cheerful voice. "You warned me that things would look different once we returned to Seattle, and now I'm forced to admit that they do."

"Caroline," he said her name with a wealth of frustration. "Don't lie to me again."

"Who's lying?" Her voice cracked,

and she struggled to hold back stinging tears as she chewed on the corner
of her bottom lip.

"Is your pride worth so much to
you?"

Unable to answer him, she stared
into the black depth of the coffee
mug.

"Maybe we should experiment."

"Experiment?"

"Let me kiss you a couple of times
and see how you feel." He took the
mug from her hands and set it on the
counter.

"There isn't any need. I know what
I feel," she argued, knowing that if he
touched her, she would be lost. With
her hands behind her, guiding her,
she edged her way along the kitchen
wall.

"It may be the only way," he continued, undaunted. "It seems that we've come to different conclusions here. There's too much at stake for me to let you pass judgment so lightly."

"I know how I feel."

"I'm sure you do." He cupped her shoulders with his hands, halting her progress. "I just don't think you're being honest with yourself — or me — about your feelings."

"Ted, please don't."

"I have to," he breathed, bending toward her.

She averted her mouth, so that his lips brushed her cheek. "Please," she whispered. "It won't do any good."

His hands slid from her shoulders up her neck to her chin, tilting her face to receive his kiss. The pressure of his mouth was as light as the morning sun touching the earth.

Soon the magnetic desire that was ever-present between them urged their mouths together in a kiss that left Caroline clinging to the counter to stay upright.

"Well?" he asked hoarsely, spreading kisses around her face, pausing at her temple.

She kept her eyes pinched shut. "That was . . . very . . . nice."

"Nice?" His hands slid around her waist, bringing her to him until she was pressed hard against his chest. "It was more than nice."

"No," she offered weakly, pushing against him.

He kissed her again, only this time his lips stayed and moved and urged and tested. Caroline was lost. Her arms rose from his chest to link around his neck, so that she was arched against him. Softly, she moaned, unable to hold back any longer, clinging to him, weak with longing and desire. Again and again his mouth met hers, until she saw a glimpse of heaven and far, far beyond.

When he broke the contact, she buried her face in the curve of his neck. The irregular pounding of his heart echoed hers.

"Does that convince you?"

"It tells me that we have a strong physical attraction," she answered, breathless and weak.

"More than that. What we share is spiritual."

"No." She tried to deny him, but her feeble protest was broken off when he raised his mouth to hers and kissed her again. The kiss was tempestuous, earth-shattering.

"Don't argue," he said with a guttural moan. "I love you, Caroline. I want us to marry and give Stranger a home."

"I thought you said you gave him away." It was far easier to discuss the dog than to think about the first part of his statement.

"No, I didn't." Tenderly he kissed the bridge of her nose, as if he couldn't get enough of the feel of her. "I said I found him a home. And I have. Ours."

"Oh." She pressed her forehead to the center of his chest as she took in everything he was saying. She loved him. Dear Lord, she loved him until she thought she would die without him. But sometimes love wasn't enough. "I — I don't think anyone should base something as important as marriage on anything as flimsy as making a home for a stray dog."

"I love you," he whispered against her hair. "I think I've loved you from the time I first saw you."

Slowly she raised her eyes so that she could see the tenderness in his expression and believe what he was saying. Her fingertips traced the angular line of his jaw.

"Why didn't you tell me?"

"That I loved you? Honey, surely you can understand why, given the —"

Her fingers across his lips stopped him. "You're an artist, aren't you?"

He blinked and captured her hand, then kissed it. "So that's it." He forced the air from his lungs. "I should have told you, but to be honest, I was wary. I was afraid that if you saw my work, you'd think it was another one of my interests, like dancing lessons, that always made you think less of me."

"You thought that of me?" she asked, forcibly trying to break free. It hurt to believe that he saw her as so insensitive.

"Listen to me." His hold tightened, not allowing her out of his embrace. "That was only in the beginning, before I realized how much you'd changed. Later, I thought I'd surprise you with the painting and make it a wedding gift."

"That's why you didn't want me to see it that day on the bluff?"

He wove his hand into her hair, running her fingers through her curls. "The only reason."

"Oh, Ted." She pressed her head over his heart, hugging him hard. "I was so hurt . . . I'd talked for days and days, sharing the most personal parts of my life with you. And when . . . when I saw that there was a part of yourself that you hid from me, I felt terrible. I lied about being bored. I loved being with you every minute that we were together. It nearly killed me to leave you."

"I knew you were lying all along. What I couldn't figure out was why."

"I lied because I thought you didn't care. But . . . how did you know?" She had thought she'd given an Academy Award–winning performance.

"No one could shine with as much happiness as you did and be faking it," he replied, smiling tenderly.

She closed her eyes, holding on to the rapture his words spread through her soul. "You're sure you want to marry me? I'm stubborn as a mule, contrary, proud —"

"Headstrong, reckless and over-bearing," he interrupted with a chuckle. "But you're also warm, loving, creative and so many other wonderful things that it will take me a lifetime to discover them all."

"I'll marry you, Ted Thomasson, whenever you want."

His gaze took in her happiness. "We're going to have some fantastic children, Caroline Lomax."

They kissed lightly, and Caroline grinned. "I think you may be right," she whispered, bringing his mouth down to hers.

The employees of Thorndike Press hope you have enjoyed this Large Print book. All our Thorndike, Wheeler, and Kennebec Large Print titles are designed for easy reading, and all our books are made to last. Other Thorndike Press Large Print books are available at your library, through selected bookstores, or directly from us.

For information about titles, please call:
  (800) 223-1244

or visit our Web site at:
  http://gale.cengage.com/thorndike

To share your comments, please write:
  Publisher
  Thorndike Press
  10 Water St., Suite 310
  Waterville, ME 04901